SPOT, THE DOG THAT BROKE THE RULES

and Other Great Heroic Animal Stories

Other books in the series
The Good Lord Made Them All
by Joe L. Wheeler

Owney, the Post Office Dog
and Other Great Dog Stories

Smoky, the Ugliest Cat in the World
and Other Great Cat Stories

Wildfire, the Red Stallion
and other Great Horse Stories

Dick, the Babysitting Bear
and Other Great Wild Animal Stories

SPOT, THE DOG THAT BROKE THE RULES

and Other Great Heroic Animal Stories

Compiled and edited by
Joe L. Wheeler

Pacific Press® Publishing Association
Nampa, Idaho
Oshawa, Ontario, Canada
www.pacificpress.com

Cover art by Lars Justinen
Cover designed by Justinen Creative Group
Interior illustrations from the library of Joe L. Wheeler
Inside design by Aaron Troia

Note: None of these stories may be reprinted or placed on the Internet in any form
without the express written permission of the compiler/editor, Joe L. Wheeler
(P.O. Box 1246, Conifer, Colorado 80433), or the copyright holder.

Visit Joe Wheeler's Web site at www.joewheelerbooks.com. Published in association
with WordServe Literary Group, 10152 S. Knoll Circle, Highlands Ranch, CO 80130.

Additional copies of this book are available by calling toll-free 1-800-765-6955
or by visiting http://www.adventistbookcenter.com.

Library of Congress Cataloging-in-Publication Data

Spot, the dog that broke the rules and other great heroic animal stories /
compiled and edited by Joe L. Wheeler
p. cm.
ISBN 13: 978-0-8163-2296-1 (pbk.)
ISBN 10: 0-8163-2296-1 (pbk.)
1. Animals. 2. Short stories, American. I. Wheeler, Joe L., 1936-
PS648.A5S66 2008
813'.0108—dc22

2008030657

www.joewheelerbooks.com

08 09 10 11 12 • 5 4 3 2 1

DEDICATION

Many an author's work has died stillborn, not because it wasn't good enough, but because the cover artwork failed to rise to the level of the manuscript. Not so with the series The Good Lord Made Them All, for from that very first book of dog stories, *Owney, the Post Office Dog,* the covers have captivated all who passed near. And this is not by chance, for the artist who

has painted these cover illustrations considers himself to be partnering with the Eternal. In fact, he told me that when he had trouble with the cover of *Smoky, the Ugliest Cat in the World* (for how could he make the terribly burned little kitten appear other than repulsive?), he prayed about it; and in the middle of one night, God gave him the solution in a dream: *place Smoky in a basket, swathe her with bright-colored cloth, then let the eyes do the appealing.* It worked! Rare is the person who can walk by that cover without stopping. Each of the covers that have followed—*Wildfire, the Red Stallion; Dick, the Babysitting Bear; and Spot, the Dog That Broke the Rules*—have spoken directly to the heart. Each is a masterpiece of its kind.

The artist, a graduate of Walla Walla College, sums up his artistic philosophy in these words: "So God created man in His own image" (Genesis 1:27, NIV).[1] Like the Sovereign God of the universe, we find joy and pleasure in the works that we and our fellow artists create. The act of creating is, in many ways, a spiritual experience. "In the beginning, God created . . ." (Genesis 1:1, NIV).

Hence it gives me great pleasure to dedicate the fifth book of The Good Lord Made Them All series to our artist:

LARS JUSTINEN
of Vancouver Island, British Columbia, Canada

Contents

INTRODUCTION

Animals Have Heroes Too

Joseph Leininger Wheeler

Where the human species is concerned, the word *hero* has been so stretched and contorted, so abused, twisted, and mangled, that it is getting harder and harder to define it.

As for the rest of the animal kingdom, few of us have even tried to define what it means to be an animal hero. Thus, when we decided to put together a collection of heroic animal stories, we faced somewhat uncharted waters.

One of the biggest problems facing me as editor was this: *how can I wisely choose which animal stories to include without really knowing for myself what an animal hero actually is?*

Consequently, I felt that I first needed to retrace the steps that led to the introduction to my story collection *Everyday Heroes* (WaterBrook, 2002), then see how many of those qualities might also apply to animals. I postulated at that time that heroes are ordinary people who rise to challenges and extraordinary circumstances to achieve memorable things. Heroes are courageous and daring. They are noble; a term once widely used but that, sadly, is used less and less today. Close synonyms would be terms such as *honorable, great, beneficent, and honest.* Heroes scorn being petty or dishonorable. In the end, it's clear that we have no adequate synonym for the all-encompassing ideal we call "noble."

Since most of us find it incredibly difficult to forgive someone who mistreats or maligns us, we consider those who overlook such injuries, even terrible acts most would consider unforgivable, to be perforce—heroes (Abraham Lincoln being a human prototype, and God the ultimate Template).

Heroes are also generous, giving, and never count the cost. They are altruistic, steadfast, dependable, magnanimous, and—perhaps most important of all—kind!

Interestingly enough, I discovered that most of the people we label "heroes" are considered such, not on the basis of the sum of their lifetime achievements, but rather because they rose to heights bordering on sublimity only at certain specific moments—perhaps lasting only minutes or even seconds. Ironically, even villains are capable of momentary acts of heroism. But people who sustain such qualities, over long stretches of time, we justifiably view as akin to demigods.

How then can we transfer these qualities to the animal kingdom? Surprisingly, I found these same qualities depicted in many, if not most, of the stories I studied—most significantly in the animals' willingness to sacrifice their lives so that other animals might live. Even more amazing—to give up

their lives, which they value and fight for as fiercely as do we, for a totally different species such as ours. Ten of the eighteen animal subjects we chose for this collection either risked their lives or gave their lives for us. Sometimes for men, women, or children they barely knew!

And every last one of the animal heroes we featured was imbued with courage, another key component of what it means to be a hero. We humans tend to consider as heroes those larger-than-life individuals who sweep through their days to the fullest stretch of their sails. Note how many of the animals depicted in this collection lived just as intensely as such human counterparts would.

We humans—a most self-centered race—quite naturally are partial to stories in which an animal cares a great deal for one of our own. Thirteen of the eighteen stories feature that kind of love or respect.

And how steadfast they are, and how faithful! As dependable as the sun in the morning and the moon and stars at night.

Indeed, as we read these stories and share them with our families and friends, we'll be reminded that God is the One who created and implanted these qualities in these species of the animal kingdom.

About this collection

For the fifth time in five years, I've included a story by the beloved Southwest author, Penny Porter. And again we feature an Ernest Thompson Seton story. Chances are, however, that few of you will have ever heard of the other sixteen authors. One reason for this is that in this collection I've drawn from the best writers of animal hero stories of the last one hundred and fifty years.

So welcome to a landmark in the lives of my wife, Connie, and me: *our fiftieth story anthology.* May it be a real blessing to you and yours.

CODA

I look forward to hearing from you! I always welcome the stories, responses, and suggestions that are sent to us from our readers. I am putting together collections centered on other genres as well. You may reach me by writing to:

Joe L. Wheeler, PhD
P.O. Box 1246
Conifer, CO 80433

* * * * *

Spot, the Dog That Broke the Rules

Carolyn Sherwin Bailey

Spot, a New York fire truck company mascot, knew the rules—knew the penalty for breaking them too.
So what would he do?

* * * * *

Spot sat still a moment, panting on the curb opposite the great ten-story manufacturing building from which flames and smoke poured in blinding, suffocating force. The dog, mascot of Truck Company No. 35, New York City, had led the three big gray horses that drew the great truck on a lively chase. It was half past ten of a dark, windy night. He was tired and winded, and his tongue lolled low from his mouth.

Spot felt, though, that his work for the evening, that of darting like a streak of black-and-white between the cars and late returning motor vehicles on the crowded streets to lead the truck, barking to warn pedestrians at street corners and to cheer his captain, was over. That the building's offices of a big garage where automobile tires were made had just caught fire in a seething, roaring mass of burning rubber did not worry the dog at all. It wasn't his affair. As he caught his breath, though, Spot looked at the firefighting, its desperateness and its terror.

The firemen were staggering from the lower story of the building, worn out and almost overcome by the odor of the burning rubber. The machine shop, run in connection with the garage, had caught now, and the oils added fuel to the fire. The men could not stand the heat and the smell of the place for too long at a time, so they were working in shifts and for short periods. The relays that came out would fall to the sidewalk, gasping for breath, until an ambulance surgeon was able to bring them back to life, and they could again climb the ladders and chance their lives once more in the smoke-filled fourth floor.

In spite of the surgeon's efforts, though, the men were dropping on all sides. A second alarm was rung in by the chief in command of the fire, and Spot watched the strange trucks and new men respond. He was a little scornful, perhaps, for they brought no mascot with them. But even this reinforcing of the firefighters did little good. The burning rubber with its suffocating fumes worked havoc with the men; and, minute by minute, the flames licked their deadly way farther and farther into the beams of the building and toward the upper stories.

A superhuman effort was needed, the chief saw, or the building was doomed. He called to the captain of Truck Company No. 35, recently overcome by the

smoke and now staggering up from the sidewalk, ready to obey orders.

"Get in there, captain!" shouted the chief. "Locate that fire; it's got to be put out!"

Followed by three of his firemen, each carrying an ax, the captain sprang into the doorway and started upstairs for the fourth floor. From his post on the curb across the street, Spot watched anxiously. The captain was his master, and Spot loved him as only a dog can love a man. He got up and ran restlessly to and fro on the edge of the gutter and then ventured farther into the road, where the engine played a fountain of sparks above his shaggy, singed coat.

Here he pricked up his ears.

Now and then Spot whined to himself and growled; arguing, it was, against the law of the mascots that he knew very well. But he also realized that he must obey if he was to keep his basket and bone in the firehouse and his running place ahead of the three big grays. It is a law of the fire department in New York City that no mascot shall climb above the ground floor of a building. A dog might, in the smoke, trip up a man when to fall would mean to die. Spot had been kicked into keeping this rule a dozen times, for he seemed able to eat smoke and flames, and he always wanted to follow his master.

He could see what was happening in the burning building as the flames, now and again, lit it. His master must be in sore danger. It was no time for keeping a law that kept him away from his captain, Spot decided, as he loped across the street and toward the flaming structure.

A fireman saw him and grabbed him by the collar. Spot snarled and showed his teeth, and the fireman loosed his grip and let him go. He passed crews of the engine companies inside, dragging lines of hose in place or leaning against the charred walls, gasping for breath; but no one saw him in the darkness. And no one heard him, for he padded his footsteps with the memories of old kicks. He was going to his master, and no one should stop him.

Spot went up one and then another, and then, at last, the hot third flight of stairs. It was black with smoke all the way. Even the flames were scarcely light enough to see by, for rubber smolders instead of blazing when it burns, giving off all the time its terrible, choking odors.

The captain and his three companions had found the danger point; it was a walled-in space that had been built inside the machine room and stored full of rubber tires and flammable rubbish. From this trap the suffocating smoke poured. The captain realized that there was only one way to stop it. He must break an opening in one of the partitions of the enclosure so that the nozzle men could get in with their lines of hose. But he also knew that his method would create a draft which would turn the smoke in their faces. Well, it was all in the night's work. He sprang at the door of the enclosure and hurled his ax against it; then, closely followed by the other firemen, he struggled into the burning room.

A mountain of smoke, more strangling and overpowering than any that they had been obliged to face, met the four men. They fell back, caught their breath, and then tried again. But the only air they could breathe was smoke-filled, and it sickened them. Once more they were obliged to turn back for more air; and as they pushed into the furnacelike place again, groping with their axes, the captain led the way, trying to reach the opposite wall and find a place where he could chop an opening and make a counterdraft, which would serve to partially sweep the enclosure clear of smoke. To follow more easily, the fireman next to him, from second to second, touched the captain's back. He could hear him chopping. Suddenly then, as he groped, he could feel nothing. The captain was gone!

He called back to the other two men to come to the captain's rescue, but they were beginning to feel the effects of the fumes and could do little more than grope their way back to the air. Then a small form shot by him, darting, arrowlike, through the gray barrier of the smoke. Spot was eating smoke, but what did he care? What did it matter that the hairs of his roughened back were charring. He whined as he hunted, and the whines sounded like sobs. Then they turned to barks of great, unbounded joy.

Spot had found his master!

With renewed strength gained from the dog's bravery, the fireman who had been close behind the captain followed the lead of the dog's barking. As he went he hurled his ax at the opposite partition of the enclosure until he was able to break a space through which the released flames and smoke poured. Then he could see the captain lying face downward upon the floor, and Spot, gasping for breath but still barking, pluckily sitting on guard beside him. An instant later the three firemen were carrying the unconscious form downstairs, while Spot bounded after them, barking hoarsely.

After the captain had been resuscitated, and the hose, turned on the danger spot, had got the fire well under control, somebody wanted to know where Spot was. He had been again whining when he struck the sidewalk, and everybody expected to see him topple over from the effects of his exposure. Instead, he was hunting among the firemen, who hurried here and there, for the man who had tried to stop him when he was on his way to find his master. Spot had decided to bite this fireman, and it took half a dozen others to keep him from carrying out his intention.

Spot is still the mascot of Truck Company No. 35. It was thought best by the entire company not to reduce him in rank because of his offense. He has been to many fires since, leading the truck and looking back occasionally to bark his encouragement. Not once since has he broken the law; but as he sits on an opposite street corner or curb watching the firefighting, there is a certain cock of his ears and twist of his eyes that say that Spot will be a lawbreaker again if his master ever needs him.

* * * * *

"Spot, the Dog That Broke the Rules," by Carolyn Sherwin Bailey. Published September 1916 in St. Nicholas. *Carolyn Sherwin Bailey (1875–1961), of Hoosick Falls, New York, was an extremely prolific writer of stories, novels, biographies, and plays. She also edited* American Childhood *from 1928–1934.*

THE SWIFTWATER BUCK

William Gerard Chapman

Once upon a time, a boy and a fawn had been friends—but that was several years ago. But now the great buck, known as Old Scarside, was being hunted by a man determined to kill him.

Only it was the boy who was likely to die first.

* * * * *

Across the sunlit swale came stalking cautiously a whitetail doe with her five-month-old fawn stepping daintily at her side; the weanling showing a curious, long, whitish scar on its flank. Before emerging from the dark recesses of the wood, they had stood in the spruce tangle at the forest's edge for several minutes; the doe searching the open with eyes and nose and ears, her fawn as motionless as herself in obedience to an unspoken command.

The mother deer was in mighty fear of humankind, but it is doubtful if the fawn would have evidenced any great terror had one of the tribe appeared, for the same recent experience from which sprang the doe's overpowering dread of man had left the fawn with as great a curiosity concerning him. Early in the spring, the doe, driven by wolves, had, in her extremity, leaped among the pasturing herd of a settler, and the cattle, alarmed by her abrupt advent and catching the fever of her fear, had raced to the barnyard. The doe and her fawn, which had followed at her heels, carried along by the rush, soon found themselves in a strange, fenced enclosure and, falling exhausted from their terrific effort, had been captured and imprisoned within a calf pen by the backwoods farmer. The man had acted on impulse, and once the pair was safely railed in, wondered what he should do with them, his first thought naturally being of the venison they would provide for his table.

The next day, however, his young son, coming early to the pen to feed and make overtures to the captives, was overjoyed by the sight of the fawn, and thenceforth he devoted himself to cultivating the friendship of the agile and beautiful creature.

One morning, some days later, the boy, peering into the pen, was cut short in his salutations by the sight of a red gash in the flank of the baby deer. The fawn had torn his side deeply, but not dangerously, on a protruding splinter, and the crimson streak in his delicate coat smote the child's heart with horror and sympathy. He lifted the latch of the pen door, which could be fastened only on the outside, and ran to comfort his wounded protégé. The doe backed into the far corner, trembling with terror, then suddenly sprang for the opening, bowling the child over in her rush. At her bleat of command, the fawn dashed after her, maternal authority overcoming whatever reluctance he may have felt in deserting the kind, little two-legged animal; and the boy, rising bewildered and with hot tears springing to his eyes, emerged from the pen just in time to glimpse the two gracefully leaping forms disappearing over the crest of a rise in midpasture. With her white flag guiding the youngling, the freed mother deer streaked for the friendly cover that loomed invitingly before her eyes, and quickly doe and fawn were swallowed up in the cool, dim sanctuary of the forest.

* * * * *

Several years passed, and in the settlements a "scar-sided buck" began to achieve a reputation beyond that of any of his fellows. Known and recognized both by the livid mark on his right flank and the immense size to which he grew, he became famous throughout the Swiftwater country. He was credited either with possessing uncanny craft or the gift of uncommonly good luck, for no magnificently antlered head was more coveted, or more assiduously hunted, than the one that reared itself proudly on his broad, powerful shoulders. And

frequently something more than desire to possess the finest head they had known inspired the efforts of the hunters of the region. His depredations on the fields and truck patches of the scattered farmsteads periodically sent irate backwoods farmers on his trail vowing to exterminate this despoiler of their crops. But these usually returned without having seen the big buck, or else, if they caught a glimpse of him, he got himself so swiftly out of sight that no chance was offered for a successful shot.

That the buck knew the difference between a man unarmed and a man with a gun was an opinion shrewdly held by one young hunter, who kept this view to himself for reasons of his own. Probably some early experience in being creased by a bullet from one of those fire-spouting, loud-voiced sticks that men sometimes carried had brought this conclusion into the buck's head. Dogs did not seem to excite any great terror in him, and on numerous occasions he had turned on those that followed his trail and driven them off. But usually he accepted the challenge and gave them an exhilarating run, and, when the game palled, broke his trail craftily and left the dogs to plod back home footsore and chapfallen.

The history of Old Scarside, which was the name by which the great buck finally came to be known, was familiar to the settlement folk. Laban Knowles, the farmer who had imprisoned the doe and fawn, and his son, Lonny, held themselves his sponsors; indeed, Lonny maintained that the buck belonged to him and always was driven to white anger by the often expressed designs on the deer's life.

Lonny desired above all things that his big buck, who only a few years before, as a captive fawn, had plainly shown his willingness to be friends with him, should live unharmed. Old Scarside, magnificent and storied whitetailed buck of the Swiftwater country, had responded to his voice and nuzzled his hand when both were hardly more than babies! The intimate association, unfortunately, had been terminated after all too brief a period, else surely it would have progressed to a thorough understanding; but the friendship so begun still held with one of the parties to it, and the boy's assumption of proprietorship on the biggest deer of the region was known to all the inhabitants of the border country.

Lonny Knowles was by way of becoming a top-notch woodsman, and his skill as a marksman with his .22 rifle was a matter of note among his fellows. Whenever his farm duties permitted, he roamed the woods, shooting what small game was needed for the home table, but finding his greatest pleasure in studying the wildlife of the great timbered stretches that enclosed the settlement. Of all the wildwood folk, the scar-sided, white-tailed deer held first place in his interest. Noiselessly he ranged the feeding grounds and runways that he had come to know were used by "his buck," and often his careful stalking was rewarded by a sight of the noble animal. His great wish was to overcome the buck's instinctive fear, in the boyish hope that eventually he would succeed in reestablishing an understanding with his one-time friend. And very patiently and persistently he sought to accustom the buck to his presence. Whenever he came upon his track, easily distinguishable by its size, he trailed him with the silent efficiency of an Indian. When, finally, Old Scarside was sighted, Lonny drew as near to him as cover and wind permitted, and watched him long and admiringly. Then, leaving his rifle on the ground, he would silently rise and show himself, all his movements quiet and restrained and his manner casual. Up would come the buck's head with a snort of surprise at the sudden apparition. Usually he would bound away the instant Lonny showed himself. Sometimes, when Lonny stood forth while the buck's eyes were turned aside, Scarside would suddenly become aware of an alien figure standing astonishingly close where no figure had been an instant before, and, snorting and stamping petulantly, with eyes and nose would seek to penetrate the mystery. Then, suspicion overcoming curiosity, he would wheel and plunge swiftly from the spot.

But gradually, very gradually, the painstaking methods of the young woodsman began to have their effect on the buck. The casual approach, unthreatening manner, and eyes that never fixed themselves disquietingly upon his own, were strangely at variance with what his experience had taught him of the ways of the man tribe, though sometimes the essence carried on a veering puff of wind would unmistakably proclaim the intruder a member of it. And as time went on, a growing familiarity with this seemingly harmless individual, smaller in stature than his other persecutors and never bearing that abhorrent instrument of noise and flame associated with these enemies, slowly wore down the fine edge of his fear. Often he would stand and stamp and snort for minutes, merely backing off slowly as Lonny advanced upon him inch by inch. Then, as a quiver of muscles rippled the sheen of his coat and signaled a break for cover, Lonny would stay him with a bleated *"Mah!"* And for an instant longer the wondering buck would tarry to puzzle out the meaning of this, before discretion sent him bounding away into the green forest depths. Later, when the buck's departure was still longer delayed, Lonny would utter soothing words to him.

"You ain't afeard o' men, are you, old feller? 'Member when you an' me was babies, you licked my hand. We're friends still, ain't we? Now, don't get skeery an' cut an' run—I ain't a-goin' to harm you!"

Awed and fascinated by the softly spoken words, Scarside would stand aquiver, then run back a few steps and halt, half hidden, in a nearby thicket, pawing and whistling, his big liquid eyes never leaving this strangely ingratiating one of the enemy kind. In the dim recesses of his brain, did some faint memory stir at the voice that, in the first days of his life, spoke to him in the universal language of infant brotherhood? Or perhaps some remnant of that early curiosity of his concerning man creatures remained to weaken the ancestral dread.

The buck's whistling Lonny chose to interpret as a reply to his own remarks.

"Remember, do you? Well, then don't be so bashful. I ain't never a-goin' to hurt you, Old Scarside—it's all because o' that scar that you got away from me when you were jest a little feller. You ain't forgotten, have you? Well, goodbye then, if you're a-goin'."

When Lonny described his adventures in friendliness with the deer, Laban scoffed amusedly at his son's firm belief in Scarside's memory of the early incident.

"A deer hain't got no memory—don't you ever believe it. He's jest gettin' used to you an' your quiet ways, like any wild critter will ef you show yourself often enough an' don't pay special attention to 'em at first. He's jest curious about you, an' a deer's as curious a critter as any woman.

"But ef he's your deer, like you claim, you better learn him to keep out o' the clearin's," Laban continued, his whimsical tone changing to half-angry seriousness as he thought of the devastated field of rutabagas he had just visited. "The pesky critter's gettin' to be a blame nuisance, eatin' up half the crops. Last night he liked to spoil the hull 'baga patch, tramplin' what he didn't eat. I ain't a-goin' to stand him much longer. Ef he don't quit ruinin' the fields, I'll put a bullet inter his big carcass!"

"Don't you never do it, Pa!" burst out Lonny. "He's only takin' what he thinks is rightly his, an' we oughter be able to spare a few 'bagas an' such like.

He is my deer, and I won't stand to have him hurted!"

Laban grumbled in his throat and turned away. The generous-hearted farmer was troubled by the knowledge that Old Scarside's continued depredations had reached the unbearable stage. Fences were as nothing to him, and his despoiling of growing crops was now a matter of almost nightly occurrence. The countryside was becoming inflamed against the big buck, who left his sign in each invaded area in the form of tracks that in size resembled those of a calf.

Leaving the boy protesting against the threat, Laban strode off on his way to a neighbor to assist in raising a new barn frame. A shortcut could be made by paddling across the lake that lay between the farmsteads, the trail to this leading over a hardwood ridge, beyond which stretched the broad sheet of water. On the shelving beach his birch bark canoe lay among the bushes, and, noting as he shoved it in that a stiff breeze was blowing in his face, he decided to weigh the bow with a small rock. Otherwise, the light craft would expose so much free board to the gale that he would have difficulty in keeping its prow in the wind's eye. Bending forward, he was about to deposit the rock carefully in the canoe, when his design was rudely frustrated. His next conscious thought was that the Wendigo—that demon of northern Indian legend which seizes men in its talons and bears them off on journeys through space—had savagely snatched at him and sent him whirling dizzily through the air.

Back in the timber of the ridge, a big, nobly antlered buck, the pride—and bane—of the Swiftwater country, had watched the striding man with arrogant eyes, eyes that for the moment held no glint of fear. The fever of the sweethearting time was in his blood this crisp November morning, and dread of man was forgotten in the swift anger that blazed within him when his trysting was disturbed. Stiffly he stood for a moment in his screen of bushy hemlock, neck swollen with the madness in his veins, bloodshot eyes glaring upon the unsuspecting interloper. Then, intent upon vengeance, he followed after the figure noisily descending the slope. His progress was a series of prancing steps, though his feet fell cunningly without sound, and he shook his magnificent head threateningly.

He was only a few paces behind when the man, reaching the shore, suddenly swerved to look about; and the buck froze for a moment before the expected stare of those disconcerting eyes. But the man's gaze did not lift from the ground. He picked up something and turned his back again and bent over at the water's edge.

The opportunity was too tempting. The buck plunged forward, his lowered head aimed at the crouching figure, and drove at it with all the power of his hard muscled body. The impact was terrific and the result startling—no less to the object of his attack than to the deer. For the man, with a grunt of astonishment, shot from the shore, turning upside down as he went, and out of the splash that followed emerged not the man, but what appeared to be a smooth brown log, that trembled and rolled crazily among the wavelets and gave forth weird, muffled bellowings!

The backwoodsman, lifted into the air by the amazing assault from the rear, had let go of the rock (which at the instant was poised above the canoe) as his hands instinctively reached for the gunwales. As he catapulted into the lake, his grasp on the birch bark canoe turned it over on him, and he found himself upright in the water, his face above the surface but in darkness. For a moment utter bewilderment possessed him; then, realizing that he was standing in over five feet of freezing water, his head in the hollow of his capsized canoe, to which he still clung tenaciously, he burst into strong language and sought to extricate himself.

With a wrench of his arms, he threw the canoe over and turned a wrathful glare toward the bank. Hot indignation choked him momentarily as his eyes fell on the author of his plight pawing the gravel and shaking his antlers in an invitation to combat. Then he found his voice.

"Ye confounded, tarnation critter!" sputtered Laban, at a loss for adequate words with which to express his feelings. "So 'twas you butted me into the lake! Ye'll pay fer this—with a bullet through yer hide afore ye're a day older, ye scarsided imp o' Satan!" He shook his fist at the animal and started to scramble up the steep bottom, continuing his abuse vigorously. But halfway up he came to a stop, perplexed. What should he do when he reached the bank? The buck plainly was in a fighting mood, and no unarmed man was a match for those driving, keen-rimmed hoofs and daggerlike antler points. Scarside stood his ground, stamping and snorting and lowering his head in challenge.

Laban wondered angrily if he would have to stand there waist deep in the icy lake until someone came to drive the buck away—and to witness his humiliation! The blood rushed to his bronzed and bearded cheeks at the thought, though he was now shivering to his marrow with the combined cold of water and wind.

In desperation, he suddenly made a great splashing and waved his arms wildly about his head, then gave a piercing yell.

The inexplicable behavior of his victim had its effect on the buck. Irresolutely he fell back a few steps, startled by the wild commotion; and at the terrifying sound that followed, his ardor for battle died. His madness cooling as suddenly as aroused, with a snort of dismay, Scarside whirled in his tracks and dashed off through the trees.

Grim of visage, but with chattering teeth, Laban climbed out of the water, beached his canoe, and hurried homeward, flailing his great arms against his body to restore the circulation of the sluggish blood. Halfway home, he met Lonny coming over the trail.

"Was that you that yelled, Pop? Sounded like someone was terribly hurted or somethin'. What in time's the matter, anyway? Upset?" Lonny gazed wonderingly at the dripping, angry-faced figure of his father.

"Yes, somethin' happened; but you needn't blat it 'round 'mongst the neighbors. An' somethin' else's goin' to happen, too, mighty soon!"

As his father related his adventure with Old Scarside, Lonny had difficulty in repressing the chuckles that rose to his lips. He covered his mouth with his hand to hide the grin that would persist.

"Tain't no laughin' matter," protested Laban, noting the action. "Ef I don't catch pneumony from it, I'll be lucky. Jest as soon as I c'n get some dry duds on, I'm a-goin' to take the rifle an' trail that blame' critter till I git him. Tain't enough fer him to be destroyin' the crops; he's started to attack folks, an' he's too dangerous to let live."

He clamped his mouth on his resolution; and Lonny knew that the big buck of the Swiftwater country was doomed.

* * * * *

The scar-sided buck, resting on a mossy knoll in the depths of the spruce wood, raised his head to a suspicious odor that drifted down the wind. He rose to his feet and ran with the breeze for a short distance, then swung around and headed back, paralleling his trail. He halted in a clump of tangled low growth a few rods from it, and waited. Soon a man came swinging along, silent footed, carrying that dreaded black stick, his eyes bent on the ground, but now and again lifting to scan the surrounding bush. Manifestly, as the evidence of nose and eyes indicated, this was the same human so lately visited with his displeasure; and some elemental intuition that reprisal was to be expected warned him that he must be discreet.

When the man had passed, the buck quietly withdrew from his hiding place and bounded off at right angles to the trail. A mixture of wariness and confidence guided his actions during the succeeding hours. He well knew the danger of giving the man a glimpse of himself in circumstances like these, but his great craft, so often successfully exercised, and his long immunity from harm had bred in him a confidence in his powers that stayed his flight to the barest necessity of keeping out of range. Doggedly the hunter followed, untangling the puzzles of the trail so cunningly woven, his skill the fruit of many a previous stalking of the wily old buck. But whereas on these other occasions he had been content to consider himself the victor in the contest of wits when he finally had come within easy shooting distance of his quarry, bravely withstanding the itch of his trigger finger, this time there would be a different ending to the hunt.

As the pursuit lengthened, familiar landmarks apprised the backwoodsman that the buck was circling back toward the settlement. This was fortunate, for the afternoon was waning; and furthermore, it afforded him the opportunity of cutting across to the runways along the ridge where, logically, the buck would pass. And then, the finish!

Laban put his plan into operation. If he hurried, he could attain a vantage point on a rise of ground commanding the flank of the ridge, and here he would have an ideal chance for a shot as the buck swept across the burning that gashed its forested sides. He neared the spot somewhat winded from his exertions, and paused a moment to regain his breath before carefully threading the thicket of young alder and birch, beyond which the earth fell away into the little valley that lay between. Reaching the fringe of the growth, the opposite slope was revealed to his sight, and he exulted inwardly as he glimpsed the object of his chase just about to cross the burned area. The deer was going steadily, but at no great speed, and though the shot was a long one, he presented an easy chance for a marksman of Laban's skill.

Without hurry, he raised his rifle to his shoulder. At the same instant the buck swerved, stood tense for a second, and began to rear and whirl about in a most astonishing manner. Puzzled by this behavior, which made a killing shot uncertain, Laban lowered his rifle to study the meaning of it. He could discern nothing at first to account for the deer's actions, and when the buck momentarily presented a broadside target, he aimed quickly and pressed the trigger. As he did so, there came to him a flash of understanding—the scene suddenly cleared to his eyes, and his brain fought to restrain the pressure of his finger—but too late! The rifle cracked, and the buck went down, and Laban rushed over to the hillside, a numbing fear rising in his heart.

* * * * *

The scar-sided buck had begun to be annoyed at the pertinacity of the man who followed him. All the cunning that so often in the past had served him seemed of no avail against this creature, who solved each mystery of the trail with such seeming ease. But he was not yet fearful; his bag of tricks was still far from empty. Therefore, without panic, he broke through the trees that bordered the fire-devastated sweep of ground, heading diagonally for the summit, from whence, in the shielding second growth that clothed the spine of the ridge, a view of his adversary's progress might be had. Midway in his flight up the acclivity, a terrifying odor suddenly smote his nostrils. He pivoted sharply as the mingled scent of man and an even worse-hated enemy warned him of danger close by, and he sought warily to locate it.

As his head lifted, his gaze fell on a long, tawny, furtive beast, crawling serpentwise through the low brush, its tail twitching at the tip, while, at a little distance in front, a small man creature lay twisted on the ground, wriggling frantically, but not moving from the spot. The stricken one's eyes bore on him at the same instant, and a cry came from his lips, cut short as he sagged into an inert heap.

Who shall say what promptings stirred within the white-tailed buck, impelling him to leap furiously upon the most dreaded of his animal foes? Whether, at the cry, he recognized the young human who had grown so engagingly familiar to him and sensed the appeal in it, or whether it was that, in the season of his queer flashes of insane courage, his hatred for the slinking beast flamed into uncontrollable rage, no man may say, but the big cat, crouching for the spring and unaware or unmindful of the newcomer upon the scene, was assailed from behind by a fury of fierce-driven blows from feet that cut into his flesh like steel knives. His spine was crushed at the first onslaught, and, turning with an agonized snarl, he was flattened to the ground by an irresistible array of stabbing bayonet points. So sudden and overwhelming was the attack that the panther never had a chance. Almost before he could realize his plight, the deep-cutting feet and battering antlers had reached his vitals, and the spark of his savage life flickered out. But as the victorious buck prodded at the now unresponsive form, a rifle shot shattered the silence, and at the report he gave a convulsive leap forward and fell a-sprawl, his nose lying against the same hand that he had nuzzled confidingly in a long-past day.

As Laban breathlessly drew near, the full meaning of the strange scene was made plain to him. A sharp pang of regret for the slaying of his son's deliverer came to the backwoodsman as he bent over the huddled, unconscious form, and saw that the child was not seriously hurt. A foot, tightly held in a clump of roots and twisted at the ankle, indicated the nature of Lonny's mishap. Thankful that it was no worse, Laban cut away the detaining tangle and gently chafed the boy back to life. In a few minutes Lonny was sitting up, nursing his sprained ankle, the pain of which was almost forgotten in his wonder at what he beheld.

"Old Scarside saved ye from the painter, Lonny, an' what he got fer it was a bullet! I'd give my rifle if I could have sensed what was up a second sooner. I saw somethin' of what was happenin' all in a flash, but 'twas too late. I'm mortal sorry I killed the critter."

Lonny sorrowfully patted the sleek, tawny neck that lay stretched at his feet. Tears were not far from his eyes, but not for the pain of his wrenched foot. "The old feller knew it was me—I allus told you he knew me!—an' he wasn't goin' to let me be chawed up by no painter!" Never thereafter, in the many tellings of the story, was either father or son to permit this altruistic motive for the buck's action to be gainsaid.

"How'd you git inter such a mess, I want t' know?" asked his father, as the boy thoughtlessly tried to rise to his feet for a closer view of the mangled body of the panther.

Lonny sank back, stifling a yelp of pain. "I come out here to see if I couldn't turn Old Scarside off the ridge, if he happened along with you after him," he admitted, "an' I ketched my foot in this here mess o' creepers an' like to broke my ankle when I fell. I couldn't move, hardly, an' then that ornery painter come lopin' along an' saw me an' started creepin' up—" He shivered at memory of the sinister, stealthy approach of the big cat; its brassy, malevolent eyes fastened with savage purpose on the shrinking lad whom, in its cowardly heart, it knew to be disabled. "I tried to crawl off, but my foot was held tight; an' I jest looked at the varmint an' tried to yell, but was too scairt. An' then I saw Old Scarside amblin' out o' the woods, like he was comin' to help me, an' I called to him—an' that's all I remember.

"You come, didn't you, old feller?" he said, addressing his fallen champion. "It's a blame' shame you got killed fer what you did fer me." The hot tears this time overflowed.

"Wonder where I hit him?" questioned Laban, awkwardly seeking to cover his own very real misery. "Didn't see nary mark, an' there ain't no blood far as I kin tell. 'Spose I might as well bleed him," he added, practicalities not to be lost sight of even in the face of tragedy. He drew his knife from its sheath and bent over the body, one hand grasping the antlers.

The moment that followed bewildered both father and son. For an instant they seemed to be inextricably entangled in a maze of wildly threshing limbs—their own and a deer's—as the "dead" buck rose in the air with a terrified snort, sending Laban spread-eagling over beyond Lonny, and, finding his feet after a few frantic seconds, sped off into the timber.

Astonishment held the two speechless for a time. Then Lonny, ignoring the pain of his foot, throbbing fiercely from the shaking up, gave voice to a yell of joy.

"Go it, Scarside, go it!" he shrieked jubilantly after the vanishing buck. "Couldn't kill you after all, you old ripsnorter, could they?" Full vent for his feelings at the deer's startling resurrection demanded nothing less than the throwing of several handsprings, but Lonny could only toss his hat in the air and wave his arms exultantly. He turned shining eyes on his father, over whose face a delighted grin was breaking as he rubbed his bruises. "You must've just creased him, Pa, an' only knocked him out fer a spell. Oh how glad I am!"

"You bet I'm glad too," chuckled Laban, "even ef 'twas the second time today the critter sent me sprawlin'! Reckon when I pulled the trigger an' then tried not to, all at once, I must've lost my bead an' shot high. Likely the ball nicked him at the base o' the antlers, an' the shock keeled him over, but didn't hurt him none. It was a rank miss that I'm proud of—an' 't will be the last time anyone from hereabouts takes a shot at the old buck, I promise ye that! Well, I reckon we better be gettin' home; I'll carry ye pickaback." He swung the lad up onto his broad shoulders and started along the back trail for the clearing; and as he strode homeward through the lengthening woodland shadows, his chattering, lighthearted burden clinging to his neck, he marveled thankfully at the outcome of the day's adventures and framed the edict he would send forth upon the morrow—to be violated only at peril of Laban Knowles's vengeance.

The scar-sided buck, plunging through the twilight aisles of the spruce wood, could not have known that from this day he would have nothing to fear from his human neighbors of the wilderness border, nor that, before many hours, the story of his exploit would go ringing through the settlements, colored into a supreme act of devotion to his youthful patron and given an imperishable page in the annals of the Swiftwater country.

* * * * *

"The Swiftwater Buck," by William Gerard Chapman. Published December 1918 in St. Nicholas. *William Gerard Chapman wrote for popular magazines around the turn of the twentieth century.*

A Little on the Wild Side

Penny Porter

*They'd hoped she'd be content to live a safe life in the ranch house. In vain!
For the little cat appeared determined to savor the full extent of the dangerous
world of the Sonoran Desert. So all they were left with were memories.
Or so they thought.*

* * * * *

Hunger stalks the parched Arizona mountains and winter rangelands.
Coyotes howl their distress. Raccoons plunder my chicken coop, and feral
dogs lust after our newborn calves. But it is the piteous cries of wild cats, solo
wanderers of the desert, that tear at my heart. Abandoned, no place to call
home, these castaways revert to a primal life and a singular culture of their
own, yet every year when hard times come they seek food and shelter in the
barns and outbuildings of our cattle ranch and farm.

* * * * *

One cold March morning, I was milking our dairy cow while five fat,
domestic barn cats rubbed against my jeans, impatient to be fed. *They don't*

even know what hunger is, I thought, attempting to count the skeletal, untouchable wild cats cringing in dark corners, cowering behind feed bins, and pacing rafters veiled in spiderwebs that spanned the barn like trapeze nets. Ragged fur of black, gray, and tortoiseshell had camouflaged these homeless creatures well against desert predators, but starvation had taken its toll. Most were ill. Many were pregnant. Some were hideously scarred, mute evidence of desperate battles for life. I counted at least fifteen, plus our five pets that made twenty cats. Somehow both wild and tame knew it was feeding time.

Suddenly, Jaymee, the youngest of our six children, rushed into the barn

cupping a snow-white newborn kitten in her hands. "It fell out of the nest its mama made up in the palm tree," she cried. "All its brothers and sisters are dead. Something killed them!"

Yesterday morning I'd spotted another unfamiliar cat huddled in the shadows behind a bale of hay. Unlike most wild cats, she was easy to see because bright white patches of fur flashed among her varied calicoes, making her an easy target for any predator. Fear smoldered in her remaining yellow eyes. She was pregnant. Today she was gone.

"I'll bet the great horned owl got them, honey," I said, wondering how the tiny creature in her hands had escaped the ripping talons and murderous hooked beak of this deadly night predator. The hours-old kitten nuzzled Jaymee's palms and mewed piteously. "You've got to find its mother," I said. "It needs to nurse."

"She's dead too!" Jaymee fastened her brown eyes on mine. "Oh, Mama, I saw her. What are we going to do?"

Jaymee had watched us struggle to keep orphaned calves and foals alive. Now she'd found something just the right size for a six-year-old, a wild thing, a precious scrap of life she could hold, love, and take care of by herself. She hugged it to her cheek and, in a voice filled with sadness, said, "Without a mama, it'll die, won't it?"

"Yes," I answered softly. "It'll take a miracle to save it."

I sighed, poured warm, foaming milk laced with antibiotics into several shallow bowls, then filled two trays with cat chow and turned again to Jaymee. "Let's take your kitty to the house," I said, "and see what's best to do."

"We have to make a miracle, don't we, Mama?"

"Only God makes miracles."

"But can't I help?"

I hugged her. "You can try."

In the kitchen we wrapped the tiny creature in a lamb's wool mitten and fed it diluted milk with an eyedropper. Then we placed it in a round, four-egg-capacity incubator we kept on hand to hatch chicks of rare breeding hens all year-round. It had a clear plastic dome on top so we could see inside.

"Can I keep it in my room?" Jaymee asked.

I nodded. "But don't tell Daddy about it just yet. You know how he feels about cats."

I, too, hoped for a miracle, but doubt filled my heart. This tiny creature needed a mother cat, not a six-year-old child. And what if it did live? Jaymee would get attached, and the call of the wild might win in the end anyway. It would take off, and she'd be heartbroken. Most of these cats were descendants of previous throwaways and had never known the touch of man. They had become accustomed to an untamed life, the life of a fugitive, in which survival depended on cunning, independence, and solitary wandering. But for now, so much hope shone in my little girl's eyes, I had to help.

Bill came in for breakfast, his wrists raked with angry, bleeding scratches and welts. "I found another litter of strays in the manure spreader," he said. "That mother wanted to kill me—vicious as any wild animal I've ever seen! And seven kittens, eyes barely open, yowled, hissed, spit, and tried to bite me like full grown pumas. I made the mistake of trying to pull them out barehanded; finally had to put on welding gloves to grab 'em, and hold the mother back with a broom." I drenched his arms with iodine after he assured me, begrudgingly, that he'd put the kittens in a box where they'd be safe and the mother could find them.

Sooner or later Bill would find out about Jaymee's kitten, so I hoped I'd heard the last of the cat problems for the morning. But no. He gulped his coffee and began again: "Darn mice chewed holes in nearly every sack of grain in the barn. You'd think our cats could keep them under control. That's why we have them, but they have to spend all their time chasing off those wild ones. They hate them. I've never seen so many . . . nesting all over the place, in the irrigation pipes, chimneys, the farm machinery, fifteen feet in the air on windmill platforms." *And twenty feet high in a palm tree,* I mused.

"Maybe if you left the feed room door open at night, the wild cats could get in and catch the mice," I offered brightly.

He shot me a quick glance. "Think what else could get in. Rain! Raccoons! Rattlers! The owls'll get 'em eventually, I suppose. They can fly in under the eaves."

"I think the owls are getting full on cats," I countered.

* * * * *

Sometimes nature seemed cruel. Year after year, these wild cats reproduced their own kind in the wilderness. They struggled for survival against predators, illness, and starvation. Eventually, they wandered onto our ranch where I fattened them up—and the owls ate them.

That night, Jaymee and Becky, her nine-year-old sister, fed the tiny kitten and returned it to the incubator that glowed on their bedside table like a miniature flying saucer with a tiny space traveler inside. I heard Becky whisper to Jaymee, "I counted twenty-two wild cats in the barn this morning. That doesn't include Cally, Whiskey, Blueberry, Mickey, or Floyd. Daddy's having a conniption."

"Does he know we really have twenty-three?" Jaymee asked.

"Not yet."

"Who's going to tell him?"

"Not me," said Becky, "but he'll find out."

Ten days later the kitten's eyes opened, and Jaymee named it Miracle. "It's a girl," she announced at dinner that night.

"Aren't they always?" said Bill, his eyebrows perfect pup tents as he scowled at me. Jaymee had shown him the kitten in the incubator the day before. When she said, "Doesn't it look like the littlest astronaut in the world, Daddy?" what could he say? But I knew he wasn't happy.

Miracle. There could be no other name for this tiny, pink-nosed, blue-eyed star in Jaymee's life. However, when I looked at her fur, white as milkweed down except for the copper patch of calico behind her left ear, I thought about the dark that waits with "stars" of its own—coyotes, raccoons, and great horned owls. At the same time, I knew we couldn't keep this kitten in the house forever.

Somehow, Miracle would have to become a domestic cat, a barn cat. Meanwhile, worries and problems haunted me. Instead of sleeping prettily in her own bed, Miracle hid in closets and behind drapes. After long searches, we found her skulking in back of the aquarium and bookshelves, in Bill's extra pair of boots, or snoozing under beds and sofas. The household question became, "Where's Miracle?"

Then there was Bill. He didn't like cats in the house. A newborn trapped in an incubator was one thing. But when Miracle was two weeks old I noticed him trying to avoid the kitten's bewitching jewellike eyes, muttering, "She's getting bigger." At last the morning came when he caught Miracle skydiving from the drapes. That afternoon she mastered free-flying from curtains to lampshades, and by nightfall the lazy Susan on the kitchen table became a splendid launching pad for a white fur-glazed rocket aimed at shelves, counters, and destinations unknown. On the day when she spiraled up Bill's jeans with claws unsheathed, life for Miracle took a nosedive. The enclosed back porch became her new home.

For a while she perched on the windowsill, seemingly content to bat at dusty sunbeams or track a leaf scuttling across the parched fields outside. But more often, I noticed an accusing loneliness in the deep blue eyes, a sudden dilation of black pupils, or an anxious tail twitching a warning. Miracle was carving dreams—wild cat dreams—of an unmapped world with all its tempting possibilities beyond the glassed-in porch.

Bonded to Jaymee from her earliest hours, Miracle seemed unaware she was a cat. "Mirry's afraid of cats," Jaymee said. "She thinks she's a person." Indeed, the kitten liked to eat on the kitchen table when Bill wasn't around. She thrilled at rides in the pickup on Jaymee's lap. She loved being brushed, but she never learned to wash herself like domestic cats do. We wondered if wild cats didn't bathe. Regardless, Jaymee gave her baths to keep her white, and unlike most cats, Miracle loved her bath—especially the blow-dryer.

Although we offered Miracle marbles, jacks, and fluffy ribbons to play with, she wasn't interested and waited impatiently for us to take her outdoors instead. Bursting with curiosity, she leaped through hay buyers' truck windows, darted into the alfalfa fields, and crouched outside my chicken coop trembling with desire at the sight of two hundred peeps. She had to be watched, and I was always relieved when the children brought her back inside where she curled up like a pretty white powder puff and purred happily on Jaymee's lap until "porch time."

In the happy hunting grounds of my imagination, it was hard to imagine that anything so precious might really have wild cat blood running through her veins, natural wanderlust and instincts that could one day tempt her to prey on baby creatures and birds. We wanted Miracle to be different, the stay-in-the-house cat variety addicted to catnip. After all, she loved being read to, sharing Popsicles, and being caressed on that patch of calico behind her left ear by a little girl who loved her. I prayed she'd stay that way, but at the age of seven months, the nighttime yowling began.

"She sees things in the dark that we can't see," said Jaymee at breakfast. "Secrets and—"

"——Tomcats!" said Bill, stiff-necked and grouchy from sleeping with his head under the pillow to block out Miracle's cries. "Darn cat," he grumbled, giving me a frosty look. The yowling grew worse. Although deep down I knew better, I liked to think the little cat was simply lonely for Jaymee.

Jaymee had ideas of her own. "Maybe if Mirry had a friend?" she suggested. "Blueberry's going to have kittens. Maybe . . ."

Bill didn't have to say no. A raised eyebrow or a steely glance spoke louder than words. We all knew there'd be no "friend" on the porch for Miracle.

One evening Bill came in for dinner with a handful of rattlesnake rattles. "We found a nest of more than fifty of the critters over at Cowan's ranch," he said, locking his rifle in the gun cabinet and tossing the rattles onto the kitchen table. He selected the biggest, a set with thirteen rattles, and shook it. Instantly Miracle's pink nose was pressed against the kitchen window. Her back arched. Flinty eyes sparked.

"Oh, Daddy. Can Mirry have one to play with?" Jaymee asked.

"Sure," he said. "Why not?"

The little cat bristled and pounced. No boring toy this. Something far more interesting. A nudge? A danger? A thrill instilled from the wild cat world? In seconds, the rattles were clicking and skittering across the slick tile floor like a hockey puck, Miracle in pursuit executing hairpin turns, her hindquarters jackknifing like our cattle trailer did when Bill had to slam on the brakes to avoid hitting a rabbit. For a while, the yowls in the night diminished as our little white cat honed her latent feline skills—on rattlesnake rattles.

We began leaving Miracle outside all day, in the hope she would sleep better at night. She did, and we noticed something else too. Instead of hiding in the daylight as wild cats do, Miracle stayed in view. Like a little white ghost, she shinnied up trees, soared among branches, and prowled around my chicken house. *Maybe,* I thought, *if we are lucky, she'll become a domestic cat after all.* Already she always came when Jaymee called.

One of Miracle's favorite places was the barn where Bill and our son, Scott, were halter-breaking young bulls for a cattle show. There she tried to make friends with our tame cats. She would always walk around them first, but her hair stood straight up on the ridge of her back, and she'd hiss. Then, feeling a little braver, she would reach out cautiously, tap a tail, and run. But her curiosity when it came to the illusive wild cats worried me. She was strangely attracted to them, drawn soundlessly into dark corners, haystacks, and high up on barn rafters where our domestic cats never went. Not a single hair stood on end. No yowling. No hissing. Instead, she seemed to enjoy a silent communication, a natural kinship, a bonding beyond our understanding before she moved on to another.

Most of all Miracle enjoyed the feed room where, instead of catching mice, she played with them until they died of fright. Then she carried them tenderly to the porch door and lined them up like Tootsie Rolls.

"See, Daddy, she's not just another wild cat like you thought she'd be," Jaymee said. "She's doing a good job. But why doesn't she eat the mice like other cats do?" She wrinkled her nose.

"Because you and Mama feed her so much she doesn't have to."

Jaymee scooped Miracle from the ground and looked her in the eye. "You'd never kill anything and eat it, would you, Mirry?" she murmured. The small white cat cuddled up in the arms of the little girl she loved and purred.

One day I discovered a round, oozing sore on Miracle's forehead. At first I suspected she'd been hurt until blisters and circles erupted on Jaymee's cheeks, arms, and around her neck as well.

"Ringworm," said the vet after examining both cat and child under the diagnostic "blue light," where the pair glittered like glowworms on a summer night. "You'll have to treat them with tincture of green soap and antibiotic salve for several weeks; and, by the way, warn Bill to watch those bulls. This strain is highly contagious."

That night when Bill came in for supper, beat, I could tell it was already too late.

"Two of the show bulls have ringworm," he said.

I thought of his disappointment, the quarantine, the extra hours of work, the cost of antibiotics and lime and sulfur dips for animals weighing close to two thousand pounds, and "the darn wild cats" that had brought the disease onto the ranch and even gave it to Miracle, who in turn transmitted it to Jaymee. I wanted to say, "I'm sorry," but I never had the chance because even in the worst of times a child's words can lighten a father's heart. "Oh Daddy!" Jaymee bubbled. "Think how beautiful the bulls would look under the blue light! Mirry and I sparkled like angels!"

It was a cold November day when Miracle's wandering wild cat tendencies began in earnest. Evening came, and she didn't come in when we called.

"I'll bet the owls got her," said Becky.

"Uh-uh!" Jaymee scowled at her sister. "She'll come home. You'll see."

Then the phone rang. "Does your little kid have a white cat?" asked a hay buyer who'd picked up a ton of alfalfa just before noon. He lived sixty miles away.

"Yes," I said.

"I reckon it likes to ride in trucks," he continued. "Didn't know it was there till I got home. Musta curled up near the engine to keep warm while I was loadin' up." A muscle flicked in Bill's jaw as he reached for his hat, and he and Jaymee disappeared into the darkness for the hundred-and-twenty-mile round-trip to bring Miracle home.

Before long, Miracle became a seasoned traveler like all wild cats. Although they might spend only a few months with us, familiar survivors returned again and again, some every year, others skipping a year or two. I felt a certain sadness because we had so hoped we could turn this wild cat into a domestic cat. Furthermore, we'd all become attached to this little white ghost of the night.

We cautioned buyers to check under the hood and behind the seats before they left, but it soon became obvious Jaymee's little cat liked touring the world beyond Singing Valley. Although cars and trucks were a favorite mode of travel, she vanished more often on foot and was gone for days at a time. When she finally came home, Jaymee exclaimed, "She's filthy! Just like a dirty, old wild cat," and gave her a bath.

"Maybe dirty's safer," I warned. "She blends with the desert." But Jaymee didn't want her to be dirty.

On Miracle's first birthday, owls were hatching, coyotes were whelping, and snakes were shedding their skins. I heard Scott yell from a horse corral, "Miracle! Get outta there!" And in the next breath, "Dad! Rattler!"

Bill grabbed a shovel from the pickup, and I dashed to the tack room for the antivenom kit. The diamondback had struck a mare between the nostrils. The horse was staggering, pawing the ground, her eyes white-rimmed with panic. In minutes her head had swelled to the size of a rhinoceros's head. She couldn't breathe. During the agonizing hour that followed, I remember spotting Miracle under the manure spreader. She looked—strange. But the mare was our worry now. We had to save her.

Not until Bill had administered the antidote and thrust a four-foot plastic filter tube from our tropical fish tank up the mare's nose and down her throat so she could get some air, did Scott say, "If it hadn't been for Mirry, that flash of white, I wouldn't have seen this happen. The cat was going bonkers over that snake, leaping around, jumping at those rattles like she wanted to play." He stopped and looked at me. "Mom, I think the snake got Miracle too."

I ran to the little cat. She lay motionless—eyes sealed, her head bigger than her body. Bill picked up the bottle of antivenom serum. It was empty. "I'll try some cortisone," he murmured. "It's all we've got."

I carried the seemingly lifeless ball of white fluff onto the porch and laid her gently in her box. Two days later Miracle was still in a coma when we saw Jaymee press two fingers against the little cat's chest like she'd seen Bill do with a dying calf. "Mirry's going to be fine," she said in a choked voice. "I think I can feel her heart still beating."

Emotion flickered across Bill's face then and, though weary from a long day, he got up from the table and returned a few minutes later with his cattle stethoscope and knelt beside her. "Here, honey. Try this." He hung the stethoscope from Jaymee's ears. Then, holding the monitor in his big callused hand, he pressed it to the little cat's ribs right where the heart should be and watched the face of the child he loved. Suddenly her dark eyes brimmed and fastened on his. "Oh, Daddy," she cried, "I hear it! Now I know she's going to live!"

Miracle's recovery was slow, and we vowed when she got well we would never let her outside again, but good intentions don't always last, and as her strength returned, so did her nomadic dreams. Furthermore, doors open and close. Cats sneak out. If only her fur didn't signify prey.

Jaymee stopped bathing her. With so little rain, predators abounded on the ranch, and we feared the inevitable. Sometimes Miracle disappeared for days or weeks at a time, only to return looking more independent, scuffed up, and dustier than ever. By fall she was gone more than she was home. Was she, in fact, returning to her roots?

"She's starting to look more and more like a wild cat," Jaymee said when the little cat returned with her first scar, a diagonal wrinkle between her blue eyes. "I wonder what she eats?" Although we talked about desert menus—bugs, birds, lizards, and rodents—Jaymee liked to think there were other ranchers and farmers who fed her the right things when she stopped by to "bum a meal," things like fresh cow's milk and cat chow.

Miracle was only two and a half when she disappeared for the last time. Another year of drought, and predators had taken most of our domestic cats as well as those from the wild. Perhaps the owls were to blame. Or coyotes?

Maybe the return of eagles from Mexico? We would never know because nature keeps her secrets. But cats, both wild and tame, had become as much a part of our ranch as the cattle, horses, chickens, and wildlife. They'd found a place to call home. We missed them. Miracle most of all.

Although Jaymee would come to love many cats over the years, Miracle would always remain closest to her heart. We had all been victims of the little white cat's subtle magnetism. Even Bill—in his own way. Yet never in our wildest dreams did we realize that hours spent in play on the back porch and feed room had been mere rehearsals for perilous acts of survival she would need for the life she chose. The life of a wild cat.

One evening, three years after Miracle disappeared, Bill came in, his eyes bright with mischief. "Jaymee!" he called. "Come outside a minute! I gotta show you something." We all followed.

Camouflaged against the weathered-metal barn roof crouched a battered little cat. Its dusty fur was puckered with scars, its right ear pasted to its skull. But the left ear, though ripped and torn, betrayed a trace of calico.

"Mirry!" Jaymee whispered, her face glowing with excitement.

All of us shared Jaymee's joy, but I also felt concern because I was sure this was no longer the "Mirry" she'd loved years before. This was a battle-hardened cat. In her world there could be no room for memories of the little girl who'd held her and bathed her and cherished her quirky little ways. Jaymee had been shattered when Miracle disappeared for those three years. Would she be hurt even worse now when Miracle failed to recognize her?

Meanwhile, spellbound, we all watched as Miracle's eyes fixed on a small brown bird nearby.

"No, Mirry!" Jaymee screamed. "Don't kill it!"

The cat hesitated. Then shifting her gaze toward Jaymee's familiar voice, she eased down and leapt into Jaymee's outstretched arms. "I knew you'd come back!" Jaymee said. "I knew it!"

Except for occasional two-day trips, Miracle roamed no more. She ate cat food, left mice on the doorstep, and seemed to settle down to domestic cat life until the morning Bill found her on the seat of his John Deere tractor. Her rugged little heart had simply stopped. She was only seven years old. "At least Mirry died at home," Jaymee said quietly, "with her family."

Yes, I thought, certain now in my own heart that even in the strangest of animal cultures, a child's love *can* overcome the ultimate call of the wild.

* * * * *

"A Little on the Wild Side," by Penny Porter. Published February 1997 in Reader's Digest *and in Porter's anthology,* Heartstrings and Tail-Tuggers *(Ravenhawk Books, 1999). Reprinted by permission of the author.* Reader's Digest *has published more of Penny Porter's true-life animal stories than those of any other author. Today, she lives and writes from her home in Tucson, Arizona.*

JACK OF SUGAR HOLLOW

Elvira Graeme

Jack came from Sugar Hollow, the other side of the tracks, where even the dogs carried a bad reputation. Now, in the cold of winter, the wild dogs of Sugar Hollow were on the attack. No one knew where they would strike next.

* * * * *

I well remember the first time I saw him—that large, black, short-haired mongrel. He did not have any beauty about him, but his small owner was pleased with him. They were pals. Everywhere one went, the other was sure to go.

That school year I went to board with Fred's parents while I taught their school. Fred often talked about his pal. I noticed that he took dainties from his plate and carried them to Jack. "You see," he said to me, "I'd rather Jack had them than I. He likes good things to eat. He's such a nice, beautiful dog!"

"Where did you get him?" I asked.

"Oh, he's one of the dogs from Sugar Hollow."

"From Sugar Hollow?" I questioned.

"Yes. He used to be a tramp dog, but he didn't like that kind of life; so he came to me. He's a civilized dog now."

"What do you mean?" I asked.

"Well, you see the folks who live in Sugar Hollow are half Indian, half French, half Canadian, half English, and half—"

I laughed. "How many halves do they have?" I asked in a teasing mood.

"Oh, many!" he answered.

"How about their dogs?" I reminded him.

"They have dozens of dogs, but I don't think they love them. They let their dogs take care of themselves. I guess it costs too much to feed them; so they let them get their food as best they can. It isn't so bad in the summer, but in the winter it's hard for them to find enough to eat in Sugar Hollow; so they go in packs to hunt food. They come across the ridge and kill sheep and calves and try to coax our dogs to go with them. They get vicious, too, and act like a pack of wolves. I'm afraid of them."

After his explanation I did not blame him for being afraid. In fact, his account put fear in my heart too.

The following weeks and months were so full of work that I forgot about the dogs of Sugar Hollow. Then winter settled down, with its biting cold and deep snow.

One morning Fred's father came to the house with a worried look on his face. "The dogs of Sugar Hollow were here last night. They tore several boards off our barn door in an effort to get the calf."

"They didn't coax Jack away, did they?" Fred asked anxiously.

"No, no," Father replied. "Jack is all right."

"I knew he was too civilized to go with those dogs," Fred said with an air of confidence as he glanced at me.

Several nights passed, and the dogs did not return. "I guess they have gone elsewhere," Fred's father said one morning. "I'm thankful they have left our community."

I felt relieved, for I had feared that the dogs might do some damage or coax Jack away, and I knew that would bring much sorrow to Fred.

That morning I started to school earlier than usual. It was a cold day, and I wanted the schoolroom well heated before the children arrived. I had gone but a short distance when Jack caught up with me. "Go back!" I commanded sternly. He walked to the side of the road, but still followed me. Never before had he accompanied me to school, although he always came to the door with Fred and returned for him in the afternoon.

"Jack," I entreated, "go back and bring Fred." Still Jack refused to leave me.

By this time I had come to a sharp turn in the road. The rest of the path led through woods where no one lived. I stopped and looked back at the last house; then I entered the woods. Jack still followed me. Often he paused and sniffed the air and listened. I stopped, too, and scanned the trees around me. I could not see anything or hear anything. "Jack," I said, "you had better go back now. Fred needs you."

I started on. Jack stepped in front of me and took the lead.

The snow was getting deeper and deeper. I had to pick my way carefully, so I had not time to look up or notice Jack.

Suddenly he gave a low, deep growl. I looked at him. He stood just before me in the middle of the path. Every hair on his ruff was raised. I knew he was waiting for something to attack him. Then I saw the enemy. Less than one hundred feet away, a pack of half-wild dogs came running toward us. They snarled and snapped and bared their fangs as if they meant to end my life. I looked for a stick or something with which to defend myself, but could find nothing.

The dogs surrounded me. Then they stopped. The lead dog, a huge, half-wolf animal, approached Jack. For an instant they snarled and snapped at each other. Then the fight began. The attacking foe was much larger than Jack, and I feared the outcome, but the other dogs merely looked on. I thought perhaps I could escape, but there was no way to break through the circle that surrounded me.

I bowed my head in prayer. "Oh, Lord," I cried, "spare my life if it is Thy will. Give Jack strength for victory."

I looked up in time to see the lead dog leap at my protector's throat, but Jack deftly dodged his sharp fangs. They fought furiously. Then there was a loud howl of pain, and the lead dog limped away. He had no more than gone when another dog stepped forward. Jack stood waiting with hair raised. When the attack came he fought gallantly, but I could see that his strength was ebbing. "Oh, Lord, give him more strength," I prayed.

Soon the second dog limped away, howling with pain. A third, a fourth, and a fifth dog fought Jack. When each battle was ended, he seemed about ready to fall, but renewed strength seemed to come to him as he had need.

At last the lead dog gave a low growl, and all the outlaw band slunk into the woods.

I started on, with Jack walking triumphantly ahead of me. When we reached the schoolhouse, Jack paused and looked up into my face.

"You're a wonderful dog," I said as I stopped to pat his head. In an instant, he was gone. Back through the woods he dashed, for he must be home in time to bring Fred to school.

"Dear Lord," I prayed in thanksgiving, "I thank Thee for Thy protection. *And for Jack!*"

* * * * *

"Jack of Sugar Hollow," by Elvira Graeme. Published November 26, 1940, in The Youth's Instructor. *Text reprinted by permission of Joe Wheeler (P.O. Box 1246, Conifer, CO 80433) and Review and Herald® Publishing Association, Hagerstown, MD 21740. Elvira Graeme wrote for inspirational magazines during the first half of the twentieth century.*

MR. TWEEDY

Anne Marie Schilling

Mr. Tweedy, a baby robin, was the most unlikely of heroes. Indeed, the fact that he survived at all was a near miracle.

Then came the long auto trip across America, during which Mr. Tweedy was to have been released to return to the wild. But Mr. Tweedy had no intention of leaving his "family." The children were convinced God had sent him to them. After Mr. Tweedy had saved their lives—not once but several times—their mother had to agree.

* * * * *

One morning in early May, a baby robin lay helpless on a path near our house in Manchester, New Hampshire. Rain and high winds the night before had dislodged him from a nest in the maple tree that overhangs our walk. Bruised and weak, he hardly seemed alive when my eleven-year-old son, David, found him and gently carried him into the house.

"I'm not sure I can save him," I warned.

"But, Mom, you're a nurse," Dave pleaded. "You can cure anything!"

Challenged by this faith in my competence, I gently forced a few drops of warm water with a bit of antibiotic medicine down the robin's throat. Then Dave and I fixed up a new nest, lining a shoe box with rags and soft tissues. My daughter, Kathy, twelve, contributed a doll's spoon for the delicate operation of feeding the helpless mite the one thing that seems to agree with most baby birds—hard-boiled eggs, thoroughly chewed in advance and served at body temperature.

Those first days were hectic, with the children spending much of their time catering to their little charge; the slightest peep would bring them running. He strengthened rapidly, and by the third day we could put him up in an old parakeet cage that Kathy borrowed. Because of the bird's constant small cry for his mother, we named him Tweetie. But later, as his tweed-colored chest fluff appeared, this was changed to Mr. Tweedy.

A painful attack of arthritis in my hip put a stop to my work as a nurse for that summer. My doctor suggested that a trip to Arizona and a few weeks in the southwestern sunshine might be good for the hip. Even though it was impossible for my husband to take time off from his job, I was so anxious for relief that the children and I decided to make the trip on our own. Equipped with a battered Chevy and a secondhand eighteen-foot trailer, we set out late one afternoon just before the Fourth of July. I was on crutches, but this was not nearly so great a problem as another that confronted us. What to do with Mr. Tweedy?

By now he was nine weeks old and almost as big as a full-grown robin. His tail feathers were beginning to form, and we knew he could fly—he had made some brief swoops around our living room and kitchen and a few short excursions with the children outside the house. I decided to free him in the yard before leaving, but because of the abundance of cats in our neighborhood, my children begged me to let him start the trip with us. I agreed. *We could just as well let Mr. Tweedy off in the countryside,* I thought, *where he'd have a greater chance for survival.*

As we headed south and began to pass a number of ideal locations for Mr. Tweedy's release, Dave made an announcement from the backseat: "Hey, Mom, I'm starved!"

Kathy was hungry too. With all the bustle of getting ready to leave, there had been no time for a proper meal. Only one of us had gorged himself. Perched on one leg, scanning the countryside from his traveling cage, Mr. Tweedy looked the picture of contentment.

I decided that a hearty meal might make the ordeal of parting from their pet easier for the children and stopped at the first restaurant we came to. But, as luck would have it, the service was interminably slow. The meal dragged on, and my children became more and more anxious about Mr. Tweedy, whom we'd left cooped up in the car. When we finally got back to him, we found him sitting on the steering wheel. Somehow he had managed to struggle out of his cage. As I opened the door, he flew to my shoulder.

What a pathetic sight he made! His feathers were rumpled, and there were flecks of blood on his beak. As he chirped in my ear, it was almost as if he were scolding me for the hard time he'd had. I felt so guilty that I surrendered to my children's entreaties to let him travel with us for as long as he liked. But no more cages, I resolved.

The miles that followed were happy ones. We all laughed and sang, and Mr. Tweedy chirped away as the children fed him tidbits that they had surreptitiously removed from their restaurant plates.

I remained convinced Mr. Tweedy would leave us. After an overnight stop in a roadside rest area, I was sure the time had come. It was a glorious morning, and I awoke to find Mr. Tweedy shaking his feathers, looking out the window of our trailer at a field of flowers and butterflies. When the children awoke, he was chirping and scolding. There was no question. He wanted out.

Once again I explained to deaf ears what would happen shortly. And once again my son calmly announced, "He won't leave us." Even Kathy, who had been noncommittal before, was beginning to agree. I decided this was wrong. They must face reality.

"All right, Mr. Tweedy—out!" I said as I opened the trailer door. There was a mad rush of wings, and the kids followed.

Sick at heart, I stayed inside to fix breakfast, but soon the sound of voices drew me to the door. Dave and Kathy were chasing butterflies, and Mr. Tweedy was helping them. First, he would hitch a ride on David's head as my son ran in pursuit. Nearing the butterfly, our robin would zoom off for an enthusiastic pass at it, then fly over to Kathy's head. Back and forth he flew, while I watched in fascination. Suddenly, all three came tearing back to the trailer.

"We gotta have nets, Mom," Dave panted. "Mr. Tweedy loves those butterflies, but he's not much good at catching them. And he won't eat them if they still have wings on."

I groaned. Mr. Tweedy had always been particular about food. Mudworms had to be chopped; flies didn't appeal to him unless they were squashed. And, given a choice, he much preferred a square of cheese or a tiny lettuce and tomato sandwich to bird food of any kind. Now the fussbudget demanded his butterflies dewinged.

We improvised two nets from plastic bags and a pair of pants stretchers, and after that I had to make frequent stops to let the children and Mr. Tweedy out to hunt butterflies. Each time, I thought surely the bird would fly away, but whenever I called the children back, our incredible robin always led the way. Reaching the car sooner than his earthbound companions, he would hop frantically along the top of the front seat, cocking his head to watch for them. If they dawdled, he flew back to them.

And no matter where we stopped, other cars lined up. "What kind of bird is that?" "How did you train that robin?" One man even asked, quite sincerely, "Are you folks connected with a circus?"

Later on that afternoon, when the traffic was heavy and my hip was aching, I pulled off the highway into a picnic area. Mr. Tweedy had been snoozing; but the moment I stopped the car, he woke up and began to flit and hop about.

We had stopped on the spur of the moment, and now I could see that the place was too small for a butterfly hunt. People were resting or eating at the picnic tables, and there were several children scattered about.

"We could walk around for a bit," Dave suggested.

"All right," said Kathy. "But let's keep away from the people."

I had to smile at her remark. The Pied Piper of Hamelin could not have had as much magnetism as the little robin perched on her arm. First, the children came running. The grown-ups followed, and soon the group had formed a circle, hiding my children from view. A hush fell, and I heard David say, "Don't scare him now. You'll have your turn." Suddenly there was a break in the circle, and I caught a glimpse of what was going on.

One by one, all the people were holding out their hands, and David was telling Mr. Tweedy to go to these strange perches. Unbelievably, the robin did exactly that! From David's hand he'd hop to whichever palm or finger was the next in line. There were some people he refused to go to, Dave told me later, and he seemed to like one person—an elderly gentleman—better than all the others. Later, this man told David that all his life he had loved robins and their songs, but he never had expected that someday he might feel the touch of one on his hand.

As we pulled away from the picnic area, I took one last look at the scene in my side-view mirror. Until the arrival of Mr. Tweedy, it had been a strictly mind-your-own-business group, with each family keeping to itself. Now the people waved and called goodbye, laughing together. The touch of our robin had, for a moment, warmed their lives.

To accommodate Mr. Tweedy's ravenous appetite, Dave had set up a regular self-service cafeteria on the rear shelf of the car. He filled tiny plastic cups with such delicacies as freshly butchered horseflies, thinly sliced mudworms, mangled moths, plus water and lemonade. Not to be outdone, Kathy prepared an equally tempting array of tidbits on the floor of the front seat. Her cafeteria, however, boasted a swimming pool improvised from a flower bowl.

Now that the robin had all the luxuries of home, and the children were completely absorbed in his antics, I was able to make better mileage. But then, later that afternoon, the weather changed. Up in the sky, white mares' tails grew and multiplied while sudden gusts of wind pummeled the trailer. Combined with the air-tug of passing vehicles, this made driving difficult.

The children realized that I needed peace and quiet, so Dave absorbed himself in a butterfly book, and Kathy wrote notes. As for Mr. Tweedy, Kathy had laid down the law—he was to remain in the back of the car. No bathing and shaking water all over us until things eased up a bit. Whenever he flew to the top of the front seat, en route to his swimming pool, Dave immediately called him back.

But Mr. Tweedy soon discovered a new way to the birdbath. While Dave was reading, he didn't see the robin sidling around the edge of the front seat. Kathy, equally engrossed, didn't notice until the splashes began.

"Why, you little rascal—you get right out of there!" she scolded, as she put her finger down to the flower bowl. "Hop out!" she ordered. And the robin did.

Mr. Tweedy was now dripping wet, and instead of handing him to Dave through the space between us, Kathy started to pass him over on the window side. Just then a freakish gust hit my side of the car. The wind blew in. Our robin blew out.

Somehow I managed to slow down the car and trailer and park on the shoulder of the road before my screaming children bounded out. Unable to walk without crutches, I could not follow them as they raced back along the highway and disappeared around a bend. It was an agonizing wait before Dave came running back—alone.

"Where is Kathy?" I demanded. "What has happened?"

"She's coming," he answered. "Don't you even care about Mr. Tweedy?"

Of course I did, but my little girl came first. "Well, what about him?" I asked sharply.

"Poor little bird," he began in a voice of woe. But there was mischief in his eyes.

"Out with it," I said. Just at that moment, Mr. Tweedy came flying back into the car. Kathy followed him.

After that, we let Mr. Tweedy bathe and splash to his heart's content while the children excitedly told me how they had found him sitting at the edge of the New York Thruway. Why had he waited, we wondered, instead of flying away? Was he stunned? Or confused by the cars zooming by at close range? But Dave, who had believed ever since he found the dying baby bird that God must have wanted him to find it, would have none of this. "If God wanted us to have a robin," he reasoned, "Mr. Tweedy could not possibly fly away!"

We planned to spend the following day, Sunday, at Niagara Falls, so I drove later than usual to reach the last service area before Buffalo. It was almost ten at night when we got there, and the parking lot was jammed. There was nothing to do but pull into the section reserved for trailer trucks, hardly the place for a good sleep, but I was so tired that I was thankful just to get off the road.

After a cold supper, the children curled up in their bunks and were soon fast asleep. As for me, normally a light sleeper, I can't understand how I ever dozed off in that noisy place, but I did. I fell into a deep and happy sleep and had dreams that were filled with music. Then, suddenly, the music was interrupted by the shrieking of a bird.

I opened my eyes and saw Mr. Tweedy flying wildly back and forth. First, he was shrieking from the top of the stove. Next, he was on my pillow, screaming into my ear. Then he flew to the front of the trailer. Something was terribly wrong.

Now wide awake, I saw what had happened. With trucks parked every which way in the area, one had squeezed right up against our trailer. The driver, nowhere to be seen, had left the motor running, and the exhaust pipe, which rose vertically along the side of the cab, was less than an inch from our open window, spewing its fumes into our trailer!

What followed was a nightmare in slow motion. Somehow I got the window shut and the other window and door open. I knew that a carbon monoxide concentration of 0.4 percent is nearly always fatal in less than thirty minutes. Kathy, to my relief, was breathing evenly in the lower bunk. I raised my head to see if David was all right in the bunk above.

"Dave, wake up!" I begged. A muffled "Hmmmmm?" came from under the covers, and, as I realized that all was well, there was a little chirp from Mr. Tweedy. He had landed on the pillow and was playing his "wake up" game, helping me rouse the children as he did every morning. If Dave didn't sit up in a minute, the robin would start pulling his hair.

"Come on, Mr. Tweedy," I said softly. "It's too early for that."

With the bird perched on my hand, I sat down to wait for the man who had left his rig beside our trailer. An hour later, he had not shown up. Finally, unable to stay awake any longer, I started back to bed. I shut the door and windows, and opened the ceiling vent. If it rained, no doubt Mr. Tweedy would let me know. Exhausted, I crawled into bed, secure in the knowledge of his vigilance.

The morning of sightseeing at Niagara Falls proved to be a physical ordeal for me, so after lunch I sent the children off on a special tour while I prepared to take a nap. I needed sleep badly. But more than that—more than I wanted the children to know—I needed relief from pain. I got out the bottle of pills that I had kept hidden in the trailer. For months I hadn't touched it. "Better to gamble on Arizona than to gamble on addiction," my doctor had advised. But Arizona was a long way off.

I sat down at the trailer table and buried my head in my arms, weak with thoughts of giving in to the drug, torn by the whiplash of my endless pain. Suddenly, softly, Mr. Tweedy burst into song.

He had never sung before, but now he was whispering little notes of a melody. Like a combined teacher and pupil, he sang a few bars of *cheer-i-ly*, and then, as if he were dissatisfied with the sound of it, he stopped abruptly and scolded himself with several brief, sharp chirps. After a pause, he tried another *cheer-i-ly*. It was both beautiful and comical—a robin teaching himself to sing! Hypnotized, I forgot about my pain. I put away the unopened bottle of pills and lay down for my nap.

Mr. Tweedy did not sing another note until the following day when we were traveling through a slice of Canada. The car radio began to play "Listen to the Mockingbird." The song had just started when I heard a familiar burst of scolding chirps. Quickly, I turned the radio low and told the children to be very quiet. Sure enough! Our robin began to trill along with the mockingbird's tune. The children were entranced.

Like a baby, Mr. Tweedy was always putting things into his mouth. In Ann Arbor, Michigan, he hopped over to me with an inch or two of string dangling from his beak. He was trying to regurgitate it, and he needed my help. I took hold, and he backed away, then stopped to allow me to get a grip closer to his beak. Then he backed away another few inches and stopped again. By the time we finished, I had in my hand nearly three feet of string. *Do all little birds get into such predicaments?* I wondered.

As the trip wore on, the endless miles began to take their toll on all of us. Kathy, the world's worst traveler, felt especially miserable, and if it hadn't been for Mr. Tweedy, Dave's teasing would have been a problem. Whenever he did something to irk his sister, the robin rebuked him with angry chirps. Once when Dave tried to get him to pull Kathy's hair, Mr. Tweedy turned the tables and nipped his finger. We all laughed, and the tension was eased.

Sometimes Mr. Tweedy's foresight seemed uncanny. Once, in Texas, we came to a huge sign that read Dangerous Crosswinds. I accelerated the car to top speed, anxious to get out of that area as fast as possible. Suddenly, for no apparent reason, Mr. Tweedy began flying around in the car. First, he was on my head. Then on top of the dashboard. From there to the steering wheel. Then back again to my head.

"What's the matter with him?" I shouted. For a moment I thought he must have been deranged by the heat. But when I stopped the car, he flew nonchalantly out the window, circled the trailer, and flew back in.

The clown only wanted a bit of exercise, I thought irritably. "Don't you ever do that to me again!" I snapped. He cocked his head at me. Then he chirped the saddest little chirp I had ever heard.

The children had gone out to the trailer to check on the tires and hitch, as they always did when we stopped. Just then I heard Kathy shout excitedly, "Come here quick, Mom."

Part of the trailer hitch was broken! A cotter pin had been sheared off, and only a quarter-inch of metal was holding the vital stabilizing bar in place. Had we continued and had the heavy bar fallen loose, it would have meant disaster.

After some makeshift repairs, we drove slowly to Amarillo and found a garage. While the young mechanic fixed the hitch, the children told him about our bird and how many times he had helped us.

"I wouldn't mind having a lucky charm like that," he said to me. "If you'd sell him, ma'am, I'd be glad to buy him."

"Not for all the money in the world!" I answered firmly.

In Navajo, Arizona, the battery went dead, and the local garage man diagnosed generator trouble, which he was not equipped to repair. He recharged our battery and, since I didn't dare stop the motor, I decided to complete our trip by driving straight to Phoenix, about two hundred fifty miles away. My only concern was how Mr. Tweedy would behave without outdoor exercise. Again he amazed me. As we drove along, not once did he flutter his wings or gaze out the window as he had done so often when he wanted to stop the car.

Regrettably, we ran into a thunderstorm, which slowed us to a crawl so that by late afternoon we had only reached Flagstaff, situated up in the mountains of Arizona. With more than a hundred thirty miles still to go, I decided to stop at a service station and have the car looked at again. The garage mechanic said that we clearly needed a new generator. However, I simply couldn't afford to buy one. I had only four dollars left to get us to Phoenix, where a check was waiting.

The mechanic recharged the battery. He assured me that this would get us down the mountains while there was still daylight, but he warned me not to travel after dark, for my headlights would quickly drain the battery. There was a rest area nearby, he said, and he suggested we stay there overnight.

As we drove out of the service station, Mr. Tweedy, who had been so good since early morning, began to put up a fuss.

"Just keep your shirt on, Mr. Tweedy," I told him. "We'll be there any minute now." But as I poked along looking for the rest area, the sun disappeared. Although there was still light, I began to feel ill at ease.

Suddenly a sign loomed up. "Trucks stop and check your brakes. Seventeen miles downgrade." Seventeen miles! If we didn't reach the rest area soon, we would be in serious trouble. The road fell away sharply on one side, so that without our headlights we could never negotiate it after dark.

Nervously, I began a slow descent as the last bit of light faded from the sky. Soon the few cars coming toward us flashed their lights on and off, a warning that they couldn't see me. When, finally, I was forced to turn on my parking lights, they began flashing their bright beams to tell me my headlights weren't on. As if I didn't know!

By now I could barely see the road ahead. I was riding my brakes constantly, not daring to gather any speed. With the trailer twice the weight of the old jalopy, the strain began to tell. There was an odor of burning rubber.

The sharp drop off the mountainside terrified me, but I tried to keep my anxiety from the children. Several times I felt my wheels catch on the shoulder. Pulling the car back to the road took almost more strength than I possessed. Close to panic, all I could think of was our crazy robin. Why hadn't I stopped when he asked me!

Just then headlights came up fast behind me. Frantically, I waved my arm, and as the car was passing me, I screamed, *"HELP!"* The car stopped immediately, and we pulled to a halt behind it. By the time the driver reached my window, I was almost weeping with relief.

After I had told him our problem, he said, "Don't worry, we won't leave you. We'll drive ahead and light your way. Stay in low gear and don't ride your brakes."

It was ten o'clock by the time we reached the rest area. The children dropped into an exhausted sleep, but I was still so keyed up that I was unable to relax. The silence began to unnerve me. Miles from civilization, in the heart of desolate mountains, I felt helpless.

At that moment, Mr. Tweedy's bright eyes popped open. He chirped and flew from his perch to my shoulder, and I felt the soft caress of his head as he rubbed it against my throat. He dropped to my hand and rubbed his beak against my fingers. I had smiled at David's childish belief that God wanted us to have a robin. And yet, ever since the little bird had entered our lives, everything had been different. Even now I was experiencing something that had never happened to me: I was suddenly unafraid, certain that my prayers for strength and calm would be answered. It had taken a robin to teach me the most precious lesson in life: to believe, unquestioningly, like a child.

When we finally arrived at the trailer park in Phoenix, the engine gave one last sputter and stopped. But it didn't matter. The desert sun and long hours in a swimming pool did wonders for my hip. Soon I was free of pain and was beginning to plan the trip back home. I was anxious to return before Mr. Tweedy's relatives migrated south, so that he could go with them. And of course, Dave and Kathy were due back at school in September.

But when we finally did reach home, it became clear that Mr. Tweedy had no intention of leaving. Given his freedom time and again, he refused to accept it. By now he was one of the family, and evidently he wanted to remain so. Months went by, and the farthest he ventured was to our car, his way of telling me he wanted to go for a ride.

Two years passed. Then, one April morning as I lay in bed, I decided to play a game with him. I put my hand inside an old shoe on the floor and began wriggling it around. Mr. Tweedy flew down from his perch, but, instead of pecking at the moving shoe as I expected him to do, he began to dance. He sidestepped around the toe of the slipper, back and forth in a horseshoe arc. Faster and faster he stepped, a tiny guttural sound coming from his half-open beak. When his fervor had reached a peak, he mounted the shoe. Quite obviously, he had mistaken my old shoe for a mate!

Every morning for the next two weeks, Mr. Tweedy continued his curious courtship of the shoe. There was no getting away from it—our robin had finally matured. He needed to find a real live mate.

One Saturday morning, he roused me with an urgency he had never shown before. Outdoors I could hear the shrill call of a female robin. Mr. Tweedy had heard it, too, and he was answering with all the power in his little lungs. Before I could get the window up and the screen removed, the female had flown away, but this didn't stop Mr. Tweedy. The moment the screen was off, he flew to the treetops—and disappeared. I sensed that at last he had returned to his own world.

Tears ran down my cheeks as I sat at the window gazing up at the empty sky; and later, when I told the children what had happened, they were heartbroken. Mr. Tweedy would be sorely missed. But not for all the world would we have wished him back. He was free, and we knew that there could not be a happier ending to our adventure together.

* * * * *

"Mr. Tweedy," by Anne Marie Schilling. If anyone has information regarding the author's next of kin, please send the information to Joe Wheeler (P.O. Box 1246, Conifer, CO 80433). Anne Marie Schilling Bouchard was born in 1920 in Düsseldorf, Germany. She later emigrated to America.

TWO BITS

Patrick Lawson

It's hard to imagine any real-life horse being more heroic and larger than life than the frontier cavalry horse dubbed Two Bits.

* * * * *

Two Bits was never in any historic battle, nor did a famous general ever ride him. The highest he ever rose in the ranks was to the saddle of a captain—Captain Charles A. Curtis. Until then, the big bay had known a dozen masters for he was one of a cavalry pool at Fort Craig, New Mexico.

It was between the 1870s and '80s. The United States was trying to persuade the Indians to stay on the reservations appointed to them. The Indians, largely Apaches, Comanches, and Navajos, were not taking kindly to the government's methods of armed persuasion. Bands of warriors still roamed the high mesas. In the vast emptiness of the landscape, a troop of soldiers could be seen for miles, but the Indians seemed to melt into the background. The old-timers had a saying, "When you don't see an Indian, you're looking right at him."

That was the reason for the forts with their high stockades. They were constantly being raided by the Indians, more for the horses than the men. Among the Indians, it was considered an act of greater courage to slip a horse out of a corral than a knife into a soldier.

It was at Fort Craig that Two Bits caught his first scent of the red enemy. Here, too, he was given his name.

Men cannot be continually on nerve-taut guard without some relaxation, and so a race was arranged one bright June day when the great half dome of the sky was filled with clouds as small and white as baby lambs.

The swiftest horses of the Mounted Rifles had already been chosen by the riders. One horse was left, a big bay. An Irish fifer boy, named Cain, decided to ride him. As they trotted to the starting line, a soldier shouted derisively, "I wouldn't give two bits for that horse."

Two Bits won by three lengths.

Six years later, Cain, now a sergeant, was to meet Two Bits under vastly different conditions.

The horse had been included in a bunch that was considered no longer fit for cavalry service. Soldiers transferred from New Mexico to Arizona had brought the herd with them to be sold. It was a seven-hundred-mile trek. At the end, the horses looked even more decrepit than they had at the start of the march. At auction, they brought about five dollars a head. Two Bits came into the possession of a new and brutal master. Some time later, Cain, then serving at Fort Whipple in Arizona, came upon the horse lying on the ground starved to the point of emaciation. A man was standing over him beating him unmercifully.

Sergeant Cain sprang to the horse's defense before he recognized Two Bits. The owner was willing to give him up to avoid a fight, and Sergeant Cain took him back to the fort. With him, he took a horse-sized problem.

Fort Whipple stood on the slope of one of the wooded hills surrounding the town of Prescott. Spread out below were corrals for the horses and mules. There were also three hundred head of cattle and a thousand sheep offering constant temptation to marauding Indians. It would have seemed that with all these animals there would have been room for one more, that Two Bits could have been easily lost among them, but every one was marked and every horse known.

Cain was fully aware that the Army would not accept the broken-down old horse into the cavalry pool, and he could not afford to keep him himself, not on a sergeant's pay. It was not a matter of selling him that bothered Cain, it was finding him a kind, understanding master.

Cain's captain was the ideal owner for Two Bits, but would Captain Curtis buy him? Cain needed money for a special reason; he had to have it. "I'll let you have him for five dollars, sir," he told Curtis, "and you'll be gettin' the finest horse on the post." Curtis laughingly refused, but Cain's Irish tongue proved so eloquent that the captain finally agreed.

During the next few weeks, the deal he had made with his sergeant slipped from Curtis's mind. He was surprised when Cain appeared with a beautiful bay, groomed from mane to fetlock, sleek and filled out—on the oats the captain's five dollars had purchased for him. Two Bits and Curtis fell in love with each other at first sight.

The horse renewed his acquaintance with the Indians on the marches the captain and his troop made in pursuit of those who had swooped down on villages and wagon trains to loot and kill. He knew the wolf bark of the Apache, the high-pitched yip of the charging Comanche that raised the hair right up with its insane clamor. He knew, too, the peaceful times when Curtis would take him for a canter among the pine trees that broke up the hard, bright Arizona sunshine into soft, cathedral shafts of light. He caught the scent of deer and bear long before he saw them in swift or lumbering flight.

Perhaps the happiest days were those when Curtis went fishing. Then the man would flick the quiet, shadowed pools for trout, and the horse would graze nearby. On one such day the succulent grass tempted Two Bits farther away than usual from his master. He was cropping contentedly when the wind suddenly said, "Danger!" Instantly, Two Bits wheeled and raced back to Curtis. The captain did not stop to question. He flung himself into the saddle, and they were off. A yelp of frustrated fury broke out behind them. A war party of mounted Apaches burst from cover and raced in pursuit.

Two Bits outran them. As the fort came into view, the disgruntled Indians slackened their speed and turned back.

A second time, Curtis was attacked by Indians lying in ambush. The shot, creasing the captain's coat collar, took both horse and rider by surprise. Two Bits involuntarily shied. Curtis was thrown. Before the captain had hit the ground, the horse froze, waiting for him to remount. The smell of the Indians was strong in Two Bits' nostrils, along with the smell of rifle powder. He could have reverted to instinctive flight, but he made no move until his master was in the saddle. Even then he did not run. He walked slowly, carefully away from the ambush while Curtis, pistol in hand, waited for the Indians to show themselves. It was as though the horse was giving the captain the opportunity to return the fire, as though he knew how many there were, that they were not the overpowering force of the first attack. It was not until rifle space was between them and the enemy that Two Bits broke into a run. Behind them three Apaches rose from the bushes, the black dots and blue crescents on their faces showing them to be painted for war.

However, Two Bits did not prove the heights of his courage and heroism when Curtis was riding him. At that time, he carried a comparative stranger on a dangerous mission.

Express riders were being found scalped, the contents of their postal pouches scattered over the blood-stained ground. This happened so often that riders could no longer be hired for that stretch of service between Arizona and New Mexico. Cavalrymen had to deliver the mail. They went out first in pairs, later in groups. Even then they were cut down.

The situation was becoming increasingly tense. Captain Curtis knew it all too well. A dispatch had been received that morning from San Francisco. The nature of its contents required that it be sent on at once to Santa Fe. But by whom? Who would venture into the heart of Apache country?

The captain advertised for a civilian rider, offering the highest pay. There were no takers. Curtis felt that he could spare no more men from his troop. There were too few now to risk sending out four or five to possible slaughter.

Then Sergeant Porter of the Quartermaster's Department volunteered to carry the dispatch on one condition—that he should be allowed to ride Two Bits.

The horse had made quite a name for himself at the fort. Not only had he twice saved the captain's life, but he had won a race which even his owner thought he had no chance of winning. It was Sergeant Cain who insisted that Two Bits be entered.

"Why that horse must be twenty years old!" Curtis had protested.

"Sure, and the older he grows, the faster he goes," Cain answered.

And Cain was on his back, as he had been in the first race at Fort Craig, when Two Bits romped home with daylight showing between him and the rest of the field.

Now Sergeant Porter wanted to ride Two Bits. He said he would feel safe with him. Curtis was loath to give him the horse. He felt that he was sending Two Bits to almost certain death. Yet there was the dispatch that had to be delivered. Reluctantly he agreed.

For three bitter cold nights, Sergeant Porter slept in his blankets under the blazing stars while Two Bits stood watch, now grazing, now half dozing, but with ears and nose constantly alert.

On the fourth day, they reached a broad military road that crossed over a low hill and dropped down to a wide, flat plain. However, a flash flood had wiped out a part of the road and tumbled rocks down on it from the hill. Wagons and mule trains had made a new path around this point. It skirted the hill instead of going over it, and a mile beyond rejoined the original military road.

Ordinarily, Porter would have taken the smoother, easier way, but now he hesitated. He could not see what lay on the other side of the hill. Unable to make up his mind, he left the decision to the horse. Two Bits promptly chose the original, boulder-strewn road. He made his way up the slope with unusual caution. Near the crest, he halted, rigid, ears pricked forward. Porter, dismounting, crept to the top of the hill. On the other side were four Indian ponies, partially concealed in the brush. Porter did not see the Indians, he did not expect to but he knew they were there. They were waiting for the express rider—for him.

If Two Bits had not chosen the hill path, if he had not alerted Porter to the danger lying ahead, the sergeant would have unknowingly ridden straight into ambush.

Porter led the horse back down the hill to the road made by the wagon wheels. He could not detour around the Indians. It would take too much time, another day maybe. But he figured that if he surprised the war party, he could pass them before they had recovered enough to hoot. He moved silently forward on foot, the horse right behind him. Then, when he was in sight of the ambush, he flung himself into the saddle. Two Bits broke into a ground-eating gallop.

An Indian pony raised its head, snorting. Porter shot it. The other three Indians jumped for their horses. Yelping, they tore after their quarry. Two Bits' stride lengthened, but he was carrying too much weight—the man, a twenty-pound mail sack, three blankets, an overcoat, a carbine, and rations for another three days.

Bullets started whining around him. One struck him in the flank. He kept on. Porter was hit in the shoulder. He fired back. One of the three Indians made a half arc over the rump of his galloping horse. The two remaining Indians fired. A bullet smashed Porter's right hand. He switched his gun to his left and fired back. The carbine of the second Indian, stolen from a dead soldier, flew up in the air.

Now there was only one Indian left. He came on firing, gaining on the laboring Two Bits and his rider.

In a final act of desperation, Porter wheeled Two Bits and shot the third Indian's horse. Apache and pony fell together. Two Bits spun around and raced on. Blood oozed from several bullet wounds. The sergeant did not notice this. He was too badly wounded himself. At last he pulled the horse to a halt, slid down from the saddle—and pitched forward on his face.

Two Bits nosed him. When Porter did not respond, the horse lifted its head and asked questions of the wind. It answered, "Smoke—and men—straight ahead." Two Bits broke into a gallop.

The guard of a government train, huddled around their fire, looked up in surprise as the blood-streaked horse trotted up to them, mail pouch strapped to an empty saddle. They ran to catch hold of the bridle. Two Bits shied, snorting. Turning, he trotted back the way he had come. When the soldiers did not follow, he halted, looking over his shoulder.

The camp was immediately alerted. Mounted soldiers swung in behind the wounded horse, waiting for him to take the lead. Two Bits moved forward, staggered—and died.

The full story of his heroic ride was pieced together from the men of the government train and Sergeant Porter. Rescued, Porter was sent to Fort Wingate where he recovered.

Granted that training might have taken Two Bits to the encamped soldiers, what made the dying horse attempt to lead a rescue party back to the man who was not even his master—instinct or intelligence?

Two Bits was given a soldier's burial under shading pines where twenty-one cavalry men already lay sleeping. Each grave was covered by stones, but the cairn above Two Bits was the largest. Soldiers passing that way never failed to dismount and add another stone to the mound in tribute to the heroic horse that wasn't worth "two bits."

* * * * *

"Two Bits," by Patrick Lawson. Excerpted from Patrick Lawson's More Than Courage *(Racine, Wisconsin: Whitman Publishing Company, 1960). Reprinted by permission of Albert Whitman and Company. Patrick Lawson wrote during the middle of the twentieth century.*

THE SWANS AND THE GOOSE

Charlotte Edwards

Apparently, the lordly swans, safe from hunters as they are, disdain the ubiq-
uitous geese, who are not.
But if that is so—what stopped the swans on that memorable winter day?

* * * * *

Where we live, on the Eastern Shore of Maryland, the gentle waters run
in and out like fingers slimming at the tips. They curl into the smaller creeks
and coves like tender palms.

The Canada geese know this, as do the fat white swans and the ducks who
ride an inch above the waves of Chesapeake Bay as they skim their way into
harbor. In the autumn, by the thousands, they come home for the winter.

In hunting season the air is filled with the sound of guns. The shores are
scattered with blinds, the creeks and rivers with duck and goose decoys. The
swans are a different matter entirely. Protected by law, they move toward the
shores in a stately glide, their tall heads proud and unafraid. They lower their
long necks deep into the water, where their strong beaks dig through the
river bottoms for food.

And there is—between the arrogant swans and the prolific geese—an
indifference, almost a disdain.

Once or twice each year, snow and sleet move into the area. When this happens, if the river is at its narrowest or the creek shallow, there is a freeze which hardens the water to ice.

It was on such a morning near Oxford, Maryland, that a friend of mine set the breakfast table and poured the coffee beside the huge window which looked out from her home on the Tred Avon River. Across the river, beyond the dock, the snow laced the rim of the shore in white. For a moment she stood quietly, looking at what the night's storm had painted.

Suddenly she leaned forward and peered close to the frosted window. "It really is," she cried aloud. "There's a goose out there."

She reached to the bookcase and pulled out a pair of binoculars. Into their sights came the figure of a large Canada goose, very still, its wings folded tight to its sides, its feet frozen to the ice.

Then from the dark sky, white against its lackluster, she saw a line of swans. They moved in their own singular formation, graceful, intrepid, and free. They crossed from the west of the broad creek, high above the house, moving steadily to the east.

As my friend watched, the leader swung to the right. Then the white string of birds became a white circle. It floated from the top of the sky downward. At last, as easy as feathers coming to earth, the circle landed on the ice.

My friend was on her feet now, with one unbelieving hand against her mouth. As the swans surrounded the frozen goose, she feared that what life he still maintained might be pecked out by those great swan bills.

Instead, amazingly instead, those bills began to work on the ice. The long necks were lifted and curved down, again and again, as deliberately as picks swung over the head of a fisherman cutting a free space for his winter rod. It went on for a long time.

At last the goose was rimmed by a narrow margin of ice instead of the entire creek. The swans rose again, following the leader, and hovered in that circle, awaiting the results of their labors.

The goose's head was lifted. Its body pulled. Then the goose was free and standing on the ice. He was moving his big webbed feet slowly. And the swans stood in the air over him, watching.

Then as if he had cried, "I cannot fly," four of the swans came down around him. Their powerful beaks scraped the goose's wings from bottom to top, scuttled under its wings and rode up its body, chipping off and melting the ice held in the feathers.

Slowly, as if testing, the goose spread its wings as far as they would go, brought them together, accordionlike, and spread again.

When at last the wings reached their full, the four swans took off and joined the hovering group. They resumed their eastward journey, in perfect, impersonal formation, to a secret destination.

Behind them, rising with incredible speed and joy, the goose moved into the sky. He followed them, flapping double time, until he caught up, until he joined the last of the line, like a small dark child at the end of a crack the whip of older boys.

My friend watched them until they disappeared over the tips of the farthest trees. Only then, in the dusk which was suddenly deep, did she realize that tears were running down her cheeks and had been for how long she didn't know.

This is a true story. It happened. I do not try to interpret it. I just think of it in the bad moments, and from it comes only one hopeful question: "If so for birds, why not for man?"

* * * * *

THE KIND-HEARTED BEAR

Vera P. Zhelikhovsky
(Translated from the Russian by Isabel F. Hapgood)

The little girl and the great bear met on a narrow ledge, below which was a great abyss. Certain death must follow!

But no—the watchers below could not believe what they saw!

Sadly, the aftermath proved the bear to have been superior in nobility to some of those who had watched the scene unfold.

* * * * *

This remarkable incident happened in the year 1847, in the Transcaucasian German colony of Elizabeththal, about thirty miles from Tiflis. In that region, bears and all sorts of wild beasts are still to be found in abundance, but fifty years ago [this account was written in 1896] it was a perfect paradise for sportsmen; hence unarmed admirers of nature were sometimes alarmed by unexpected encounters. It was regarded as an ordinary, everyday occurrence to run across a bear, especially at the season when berries, fruits, and grapes were ripe in gardens and forests. All inhabitants, even the summer residents in the villas, who had come for refreshment to the villages, colonies, and military settlements in the vicinity of the capital of Georgia (which was deserted from June to September), knew this very well, and did not run the risk of going unarmed to work or on pleasure parties. It is well-known that

even women and children, in that region and in those days, understood how to handle daggers and firearms.

But it sometimes happened that weapons, even firearms—which were far from having the long range which they now possess—proved unavailing, powerless to save the victims.

This is an account of an original scene, exactly like a fairy tale which was enacted once upon a time, in the outskirts of the Elizabeththal colony, before the eyes of a number of people who were riding to the forest on a picnic, and a party of the colonists, who were returning from their work. The colonists were descending from the opposite mountains, and the horsemen were riding along the bottom of the ravinelike valley on the bank of a turbulent mountain stream. On the right hand, where lay the planted fields, grew bushes and small trees; but on the left bank of the stream rose the barren cliffs, which became more steep and perpendicular as they increased in height. At their summit, just below their last, jagged crest, which seemed inaccessible and rose in peaks like the walls of a fortress, a mountain path descended. It wound like a narrow ribbon around a vast crag which thrust forward its granite bosom. The inhabitants had broken it through the thickets for the purpose of communicating with the mountain villages. In some places this footpath was a fathom [six feet] wide; but just at that point on the cliff, it had been hard to blast it out with powder, and it was so narrow that it was difficult, not only for mules but even for small donkeys and people, when they met upon it, to pass each other. Even pedestrians generally halted behind the projecting crag, and did not enter upon that strip until they had shouted vigorously, thereby giving notice to anyone who might chance to be on the other side, so that they might not meet at dangerous and impassable points.

On both sides of the cliff, springing from the rifts, clinging and intertwining from summit to base, grew a mantle of barberry, raspberry, and thorny blackberry bushes of that region, with their rich clusters of fruit, which at a distance looked more like grapes, and nearby more like huge mulberries, than like the squat, bluish, sour berry which is called a blackberry in Russia.

The children—little Tartars from the mountain villages and little Germans from the colony—in company with the goats, had broken many a path along the steeps of the clefts nearest to the exit from the gorge; but they rarely peeped farther into it, because they were afraid of wild beasts. There was no making one's way through the wild game there.

The little path ran to the left; on the right, along the mountains, the forest began in a thick mass, cut by such deep ravines, by such crevices and jagged ridges of rocks, that the foot of man probably had never trodden them at all; certainly not in the days of which we are speaking.

From these forest-clothed vales crept unbidden guests in search of fruits and, sometimes, of living food—wolves, bears, jackals, wildcats, even hyenas, that had come from Persia or Anatolia.

When the villa residents of those days, who lived in the colonies or in the regimental headquarters, set out upon an expedition to the forest, they always sent men on ahead to clear the way. The noise of the cavalcade, the firing by the escort, frightened away the creatures of the forest, and thus rendered the place safe for the members of privileged society. Never were picnics and riding parties in such vogue, half a century ago, as in the Caucasus and in Georgia; but people rarely ventured upon them without these preliminary precautions, so that the little company which had, in the present instance, assembled for a picnic, appointed at a spot two or three versts [nearly two-thirds of a mile] from Elizabeththal, had not the slightest expectation of encountering a wild beast.

Suddenly, one of the ladies, on raising her eyes to the summit of the cliff, which we have described, on the opposite side of the rushing river, uttered an exclamation and drawing rein, called general attention by pointing with her whip. Men and women all halted and gazed in silence to the distant spot which she indicated.

There, on the narrow path which has been mentioned, with slow and stately tread, swaying his dark, heavy body about on all four feet, a huge bear was wending his way.

Apparently Míshenka (as the Russians call a bear) was either sad or was thoughtfully considering some difficult problem or simply had overloaded his stomach by eating his fill of herbs and grasses, which at that season of the year were abundant—red, green, and yellow. Like a tortoise, he barely moved; his muzzle was hanging close to the ground and swinging lazily, as though he were burdened with its weight.

For several minutes the interested spectators watched in silence the unusual sight of a bear on a leisurely ramble, and then all began to talk at once. Some were sorry that they were so far away—no bullet would reach the peak from such a distance; others wondered whence he had come and whither he was bound; others were already concocting a plan for a future hunt, coveting poor "General

Toptygin" [as near a translation as can be given for the title of Bruin], who calmly continued his stroll, neither hearing nor seeing his sworn enemies, and not suspecting their evil designs against his person. At the moment he was, evidently, in a most blissful state of mind, cherishing no evil thought against anyone, peaceably digesting the forest fruits and berries, and perhaps, also, the juicy products of the colonists' vineyards, to which he had been treating himself.

With a laugh, one of the riding party, a colonel, made the suggestion, in the hearing of all, that it would be a good thing to hit "His Waggleship" with a bullet.

"You can't reach him from here with any gun," objected another.

"Nevertheless, we might try," suggested the ladies.

"Of course, we might try! Perhaps he would quicken his pace."

"At least, let's knock the arrogance out of him! Hurry him up! Let's see how he'll run! That would be fun!"

"What fun it will be! You're bold enough at a distance; but what if we were riding on that side of the river? It's not pleasant to meet such fellows."

"And on such a path, to boot—where there's no getting out of the way. You would either have to leap into the abyss head foremost or fall victim to the teeth and claws of that beast!" exclaimed others, excited by a spectacle which was not on the program of amusements for their picnic.

"Well, after all, why not? Mikháil Ivanitch [Russian term for a bear] will not feel our shot, but he'll hear it. It will startle him, and we shall see the result," said one military man decisively, to the satisfaction of the ladies.

And, turning to a Kazakian in the escort, one of the party gave the order: "Come now, brother, try to hit that lazy, shaggy fellow; fire a shot!"

In an instant the Kazak had unslung the gun from his shoulder and was taking aim, when suddenly, from behind the riders, a restrained but authoritative shout rang out from the midst of a group of Germans who were descending on the other side of the gorge, and whom they had not, up to this moment, perceived.

"Don't fire, gentlemen!" the voice cried in German. "Stop! Don't fire!"

"What's the matter? Why not fire?" all exclaimed, addressing the colonists, after ordering the Kazak not to fire just yet and comprehending that there must be some reason for such a command.

All four of the Germans, who were walking with their pitchforks and rakes on their shoulders, halted two or three fathoms higher up than the riders, and all, except the man who had hailed them and who hastily approached them, stared intently upward, with expressions of dumb terror on their faces.

What terrible thing do they see yonder? was the general thought of both the men and women. And they, also, raised their eyes aloft.

The bear was still proceeding along the path with his former rolling gait. That was all they could see.

Meanwhile, the German who had stopped the shot had caught up with the colonel who had given the order to fire, brought him to a halt, and hastily explained something to him. The roar of the river prevented many below from hearing distinctly what the matter was, but those nearest groaned, and immediately, in affright, communicated the news to the rest.

"He says that they have discovered up yonder some man or other, who is descending the path from the other direction. He says that they could not make it out clearly, because of that projecting cliff—but that they distinctly perceived a human figure moving directly toward the bear."

"Oh, but now we *must* fire! We must call the man's attention to us and warn him to turn back—to go no farther."

"On the contrary!" this adviser was answered. "These people think that if we let the bear alone he'll probably turn off through the ravine yonder—do you see? The Germans declare that he probably has his den there."

"But what if he does not turn off there? If he goes straight on he will meet the man on the narrowest part of the path—what then?" several exclaimed at once.

"If we scare him with a shot, he will set out on a run, thinking that he is being pursued, and pass his den. In that case they will meet."

"Oh, what a terrible situation! And there is no way to help!"

"Perhaps these Swabians [Germans] have already devised some method. They seem to have an idea."

"Look, look! Those up above are pointing!"

In fact, the colonists who had remained above and who were able to see farther along the mountain path than was possible from the bottom of the gorge, suddenly began to move frantically, to talk together in haste, pointing out something to each other, and exhibiting plain evidences of being overwhelmed with terror and excitement.

All the members of the riding party, also seized with involuntary terror, kept their eyes steadfastly fixed on the cliff in expectation of what was coming.

What horrible sight were they about to see?

And, all at once, a simultaneous cry of pity, terror, horror, broke from all. From behind the crag a little girl made her appearance. The tiny colonist was seven or eight years old, not more. She was strolling along with her arms crossed carelessly on her pink apron. A large hat of coarse straw, such as all the colonists, whether young or old, wear in hot weather, had fallen quite over on the nape of her neck; and surrounded by this aureole, all flooded with sunlight, the poor little thing stepped out on the path which skirted the cliff on the brink of the abyss.

The poor child was going to her death in plain sight of many men and women—and to what a dreadful death! No one could either save her or warn her of her danger.

All were condemned to gaze helplessly at the dreadful event which was on the point of happening before their eyes.

The women raised a cry and fell to weeping. The men, even those who had been in battle more than once, who had beheld death and blood, said afterward that they became cold and dizzy, and many turned away their eyes in anguish. But those who endured the ordeal, on the other hand, beheld a marvel.

Because of the turn in the path, the child could not see the terrible fellow traveler who was coming to meet her. She only caught sight of that dark brown shaggy mass at the moment when it almost came in contact with her. The huge beast completely blocked her road. His left paws stood on the very edge of the path, while with his right side he almost rubbed the cliff. They caught sight of each other almost at the same moment.

Probably a cry or an exclamation on the part of the child revealed her presence to the beast, as he was walking along with his muzzle and eyes drooped earthward. They stared fixedly at each other. The little girl was petrified with fear; the bear halted in indecision, no doubt much astonished, if not frightened. For one moment, probably, it reflected, *What am I to do now?* It was impossible to pass without crushing the unexpected obstacle, without striking it or hurling it into the abyss. The path was so narrow at this point that he could not even turn around on all fours. What was to be done?

Down below the people waited with bated breath, expecting at any moment to see the unhappy child pushed into the abyss. But evidently that was not the way in which full fed and therefore good-natured Mikháil Ivanitch, "General Toptygin," had settled the problem. He wished neither death nor harm to this tiny creature, helpless before him with open mouth and staring eyes, having lost through fear all power of crying, and awaiting his will in trembling silence. And Míshenka carried out his will.

With a faint growl, caused not by anger but by the necessity of putting himself to trouble, he reared up on his hind legs, strode close up to the little girl, and, bracing his back against the cliff, clasped his forepaws around her, just beneath the shoulders.

Shrieks and groans of despair resounded from below. The ladies, who still continued to gaze with dim eyes, grew faint; but the men, especially the huntsmen, who were acquainted with the murderous habits of the bear family, yet cherished a hope—a faint hope—for the child's safety. They perceived that Míshka was behaving in a very remarkable manner, with all the caution and dexterity which he could command.

They were not mistaken as to his unprecedented goodness. The kind-hearted bear lifted the little girl up, carefully bore her over the precipice, and, turning on the pivot of his hind paws, set her down on the other side of the path.

Having performed this gymnastic exercise, the bear, without waiting to be thanked (evidently he was well acquainted with the human race), whirled about, dropped on all fours, and proceeded quietly on his way, swaying from side to side, and grunting contentedly in anticipation of sweet repose in his lair not far away.

The colonists hastened to the spot and found the little German child safe and sound, but greatly frightened by her waltz with such an unusual partner. But I must confess, to the shame of the men, that the virtuous bear was not in error as to his bad opinion of us. I know not whether he slept sweetly after his humane act, but I do know for a fact that it was his last night in this transient vale of ingratitude and evil. On the following morning a hunting party set out after him, and a month later his magnificent skin lay in Tiflis, in the private study of one of the witnesses to this miraculous scene.

* * * * *

"The Kind-Hearted Bear," by Vera P. Zhelikhovsky (translated from the Russian by Isabel F. Hapgood). Published October 1896 in St. Nicholas. *Isabel F. Hapgood (1850–1928), born in Boston, was an author and journalist. She specialized in translating Russian stories and books.*

GOLDEN ARROW

Mary Ethel Oliver

Little Tong had appendicitis. Unless help came soon—very soon—the little boy was doomed.
So what could they do?

* * * * *

The slap of wind in her face was refreshing, but Fay Meredith had a frown of worry on her usually merry face as she leaned over the rail of the *Elsbeth*. Off in the southwest, there was a beautiful woolly cloudhead; but Fay knew how quickly those opalescent cloudheads could pile up and turn dark, how soon they could spread over the sky and spill torrents of rain and wind.

"That certainly doesn't look like fair weather ahead," she told her cousin, Jimmy Taylor, as he came up beside her.

Jimmy was first mate of the trim cruising yacht that was owned and captained by his father, and now his eighteen years and a jaunty cap made him look very wise and nautical.

"Don't let that bunch of wool on the horizon scare you," he laughed. "The *Elsbeth* has ridden through a good many squalls."

Right now Jimmy was all sailor. No doubt he had already completely forgotten that Fay was not taking this trip for pleasure and that even after the

Elsbeth was safely docked at Woodward Wharf the weather would be something for Fay to worry about—for Fay and at least fifty others.

Yes, it was natural that Jimmy should think first of what would happen to the *Elsbeth* in a storm. Just as it was natural for Fay to think of what would happen to Golden Arrow and Starlet—the best birds in her flock of homing pigeons. They were at this moment preening themselves in a cage on the aft deck, quite enjoying their voyage. The pigeons and Fay were bound for the annual race at Woodward. This year Fay had high hopes of winning one of the cash prizes with Golden Arrow, who had come in third the previous year. Starlet, she was entering chiefly for the sake of training. She hoped this first race of Starlet's would be a stepping-stone to prize-winning prowess in future years.

Pigeons as well as yachts could fight their way through storms, she knew; but she did not want her pets to have to battle a storm for the fifty miles of the race.

Fay strolled down the deck to the pigeon cage. First Starlet, then Golden Arrow, she took out to stroke and talk to. Jimmy, watching, smiled apologetically and came toward her again.

"I see," he said. "It's the champs to be that you're worried about; but you needn't be afraid, Fay. There may be a squall coming, but it'll be over long before the start of the pigeon races."

"You really think so, Jimmy?"

"Sure, these sudden blows don't last long." He stroked Golden Arrow's shining back. "So this is the one that's going to come in first, you hope?"

"I hope," replied Fay. "If Golden Arrow only knew what five hundred dollars could do for the Merediths!"

She laughed lightly. Not even to Jimmy, who had known some struggles himself, could Fay bring herself to divulge how long the Meredith farm had waited for needed repairs, how many times Mother and Dad had denied themselves small luxuries in order to buy things for herself or her two brothers.

Three years ago her older brother had decided to try to help the family by raising pigeons for breeders and fanciers, but not many months had passed before he had come to the conclusion that his venture was unprofitable. So Fay had taken over Ted's pigeons as a hobby, still hoping that someday it might prove to be a profitable one. Now she smiled down at the champion of her flock as he nestled in the crook of her arm.

"He averaged fifty-two miles an hour in the last three tests," she told Jimmy proudly. "Last year's winner clocked only fifty!"

Jimmy expressed his admiration in a long whistle. "You were right when you picked a name for him then."

A sudden chill gust ruffled Golden Arrow's feathers. Fay placed him back in his cage and carried it down the companionway to a sheltered corner of the after cabin. As she was returning to the deck, Wah Ling, the cheerful cook of the *Elsbeth,* sped past her with only a fleeting smile of greeting.

"What's wrong with Ling?" Fay asked her Aunt Beth as she stepped out of one of the staterooms.

"Is there something wrong with Ling?" Aunt Beth asked, surprised and concerned.

"He just went past me as though something was after him."

They heard a porthole bang shut somewhere forward, and both women looked relieved.

"He was probably just seeing that we don't get wet," declared Fay. "Jimmy says there's going to be a bit of a squall."

"But why isn't young Tong attending to the portholes?" wondered Aunt Beth. "Ling has enough to keep him busy in the galley this close to lunch hour."

Her sentence was hardly finished when Wah Ling came dashing down the narrow corridor again, his eyes wild with panic.

"My lil' Tong! Him got awful big pain. Alla time him holla! Missy, you come?"

Mrs. Taylor was already on her way to the tiny aft stateroom where the little Chinese boy shared quarters with his father. In a few moments, she was back beside Fay.

"Run, get Jimmy quickly! Tell him to take the wheel and send his father down here. Little Tong is very ill. Hurry!"

Although there were a dozen anxious questions on the tip of her tongue, Fay did not pause to ask them but turned and sped up the companionway.

Five minutes later, she and her aunt were waiting silently outside the little stateroom door when Captain Taylor stepped out. His expression was grave.

"Appendicitis," he said briefly. "He's beyond the point where I can help him. We'll have to put into port and get him to a hospital."

"How far is the closest port?"

"Point Knoll, thirty miles south. I'm not sure we can get through the straits with the wind that's kicking up, and the current is against us. But we'll have to risk it."

"But, Uncle Jim, that will take over an hour!"

"Much more, probably. Poor youngster! Beth, this is the last trip I'll take without some sort of wireless equipment."

Fay stared into her uncle's worried face. "Wireless equipment!" she repeated. "How could that help in a case like this?"

"We could wire for help. The *Lesta,* one of the speediest Coast Guard patrol boats, is probably within a few miles of us, but we've no way to reach her!"

"But we have, Uncle. Golden Arrow!"

Captain Taylor's face lit with interest, but only for a moment. "Golden Arrow would fly back to Willowvale," he objected.

"Of course. But we could send a message with him. Mother or Ted will be sure to see him come in. One of them could phone the Coast Guard station to signal the *Lesta*!"

"But the race, Fay. You were counting on Golden Arrow—"

"What does the race matter if little Tong can be spared even half an hour's suffering? Please let me try it, Uncle Jim!"

Captain Taylor looked up quickly. "You're a grand girl, Fay. Go ahead!"

* * * * *

It took but a few moments for Fay's practiced hand to find the right size paper, to scribble a message, and to tuck it under her favorite's wing. In another moment she and her aunt were out on deck. Uncle Jim had returned to Tong's bedside to do what he could for the suffering child.

Fay gave Golden Arrow one or two encouraging strokes, lifted him high, and set him free. There was a quick whir of wings. The bird flew straight up, circled once, and then darted off as swiftly and surely as though he was aware of the urgency of his mission.

Fay felt Aunt Beth's eyes searching her face as the message bearer became a tiny speck and then faded into the mist. She did not have to force a smile. The thrill of pride that surged through her was greater and more satisfying than any she had felt when she had set free her birds at the start of a race.

"He'll make it," she said confidently. "He'll get in ahead of the storm."

Aunt Beth gave her a quizzical, approving smile. "You *are* a grand girl, Fay. I know how much that prize would have meant to you."

Fay's lips twitched. "Well, there's next year," she said, a little hoarsely. "By that time Starlet may be a winner too," and then her voice quickened with vitality. "Isn't there something more we can do for Tong?"

"You mustn't worry. Uncle Jim can make him as comfortable as circumstances will allow. He's had some medical training, you know. I'll go below again and see what I can do. You watch here, dear, and let us know the moment any sign of the *Lesta* appears."

As Fay's excitement ebbed, she became freshly aware of the rising wind and the bank of ominously black clouds that were spreading rapidly over the sky.

She glanced toward the helm and caught Jimmy signaling her urgently, so she staggered along the deck toward him.

"Tell me, what's all the stir about?" he asked. "Why did you send your pigeon home?"

"Little Tong is ill," she told him briefly. "Uncle Jim says it's appendicitis— a surgical case. He thinks the *Lesta* is cruising near us. I've sent Golden Arrow with a message asking Ted to phone the Coast Guard station to wire the cutter or send help. If they can, we may be able to get Tong ashore before the storm hits us. Otherwise, we . . . we'll have to tackle the straits and put Tong ashore at Point Knoll."

"It would be sheer madness to try to take the *Elsbeth* through the straits in the teeth of a gale," said Jimmy.

"We have no choice, Jimmy, if the Coast Guard doesn't show up."

Fay glanced at her watch. Only five minutes had elapsed since Golden Arrow had darted off. Another five minutes crept by while Fay divided her time between an anxious study of the cloud banks tumbling across the sky and visits below to get reports from the sickroom.

"Is he much worse?" Fay asked tensely.

"Ling should have told us of the child's illness long before he did," was Aunt Beth's terse answer.

"Poor Ling didn't want to worry us," said Fay. "Probably thought it was just a stomachache. Isn't he going to be all right?"

"Don't you fret yourself, dear. You've done the best you could to help."

But from Aunt Beth's tone Fay feared that even the *Lesta* could not be of much help if it did not arrive very soon. And another fifteen minutes, at least, must elapse before she could even hope to sight the cutter.

Hardly had the thought crossed her mind when they heard an excited shout from Jimmy, and almost simultaneously the roar of a motor was audible above the wail of the rising wind.

Fay rushed to the deck again just in time to see a plane dip low over the yacht, then rise to circle broadly, and then begin a long glide toward the water.

"It's a Coast Guard plane!" shouted Jimmy. "The answer to Golden Arrow's message!"

"Why it—it couldn't be," gasped Fay.

But it was. They all realized it even before the big hydroplane struck the water close by and began to taxi toward the yacht. The pilot put his head out of the cockpit as soon as he was within hailing distance and shouted, "Where's the patient?"

To Fay it was just another of those incredible episodes that come with startling suddenness and are completed and past before one has had time to feel the reality of their happening.

It seemed but a few minutes from the time that the Coast Guard ambulance plane had hit the water until it was taking off again with Tong and Ling aboard.

As the plane became a diminishing silver speck on the horizon, the three Taylors stood beside Fay, half tearful, half smiling with the fullness of emotion that comes from relief after a strain.

"Somehow I think they'll manage to save him," the *Elsbeth*'s captain said huskily.

Fay gave him a quick, searching glance. "You mean—"

Uncle Jim Taylor slipped an arm over her shoulder. "I mean that saving little Tong's life has become a matter of minutes," he said, "but, thanks to Golden Arrow and the promptness of the Coast Guard, I think it can be done."

* * * * *

When Fay had let loose her champion racing pigeon, she had thought only of possible aid for a suffering child. When she heard three days later that Tong had come safely through his operation and was well out of danger, she felt that her reward was complete. But the episode was not finished.

Golden Arrow, according to Ted (who had slipped the racing band from the bird's leg into an automatic timing device upon his return to the loft—"just for the sake of record"), had clocked a flying speed of sixty miles per hour, judging the distance flown to be ten miles. Although the record could not be accepted officially, it was not important to Golden Arrow's reputation at that point; for, hours before the start of the races at Woodward, Golden Arrow had become a public hero. The Coast Guardsmen and surgeons who were the real heroes of the incident laughingly deprecated their part in the saving of little Tong and made a great story of Golden Arrow's race against the storm.

Months later when Fay was checking up an order for ten pairs of eighteen-week-old carrier pigeons for a large news photo agency (one of many such orders that were coming in almost daily now), she glanced affectionately at Golden Arrow, perched atop his loft, crooning with contentment and self satisfaction.

"Croon away, ambassador," she laughed. "You have the right to!"

Ted, coming up the steps in time to hear her, shifted a puzzled glance from Fay's beaming face to the pigeon.

"Ambassador?" he repeated inquiringly.

"Honorary title," Fay smiled. "Golden Arrow could have won a dozen races without attracting a great deal of attention; but he helped to save a life and brought a world of public interest and goodwill to Willowvale loft. Don't you think he deserves an honorary title?"

And she walked over to offer a handful of fresh grain to Ambassador Golden Arrow.

* * * * *

"Golden Arrow," by Mary Ethel Oliver. Published April 2, 1939, in Girls' Companion. *Reprinted by permission of Joe Wheeler (P.O. Box 1246, Conifer, CO 80433) and David C. Cook, Colorado Springs, CO. Mary Ethel Oliver wrote for popular and inspirational magazines during the first half of the twentieth century.*

BRIAN BORU

Stephen Chalmers

Eighty years ago, an English foxhound, needing a boy to roam the California hills with, adopted the first one he came across. Little did Brian realize the debt he'd soon owe to his new friend.

* * * * *

The first time Brian saw the dog was just after he had left the house overlooking the Pacific and as he crossed the coast highway which worms its way, dodging foothills here and sea bluffs there, all the way from San Francisco to San Diego.

The dog looked like a mongrel. Although Brian did not know it then, it was the most glorious mongrel in all dogdom—the English foxhound which somebody has said is no kind of dog at all, because it has been evolved through centuries by sportsmen seeking to develop three things: speed, sense of smell, and high intelligence. This is why it has been termed, by those who know dogs, the glorious mongrel!

But it looked very inglorious that day. It had the appearance of being half starved. Splotches of dried mud and certain half-healed bruises and cuts on the once-white coat, which had black and tan markings about the head, suggested that it had recently emerged from a series of violent dogfights.

Brian did not consciously think these things. He only noticed, as any lad will, a dog which came toward him with a long and very dusty tail waving a friendly greeting. It sniffed at his knees, seemed to like the faint odor of sagebrush clinging to the khaki, and perhaps it understood from the knapsack and blanket bandolier that Brian was off for an outing of some sort. Looking up into the boy's face that dog seemed to say, *Ah! Here's a lad after my dog's heart! He loves the outdoors. He's off now—with a blanket roll. That means overnight camp in the open. I'll go along with him!*

Which the dog did, although it was half an hour before Brian, striking the trail for the rolling coast hills of springtime California, discovered that that dog did not just happen to be traveling the same way, but was actually accompanying *him.*

With a pleasant thrill of delight, he realized that for some reason this dog had decided that it liked him. For the time being, at least, it had elected him worthy to be its master; and no boy—no man, for that matter—but feels proud to be so chosen, even by a mongrel, glorious or inglorious.

Clearly, from the way it ranged with its nose to the ground, this dog was a hunter. Brian suffered a pang of fear that as soon as it discovered that *he* was not a hunter, that he loved wild things too much to do anything more than study their interesting ways, his newfound companion would desert him.

And then the very thing he feared, happened—part of it, at least. The dog had been foraging ahead, its nose investigating every bush and hole. Suddenly it stopped a few yards from a clump of cactus and stood as if petrified, its left paw slightly raised and seeming to point at the cactus. Brian stopped too. He had never seen a hunting dog "point." What would it do next? It did nothing— just stood there with its paw uplifted, as if both dog and paw had been arrested in midaction and frozen stiff.

Then the ludicrous thing happened. Brian, himself, did nothing, because he did not know what this dog expected him to do. He just stood there waiting for the hunter to make the next move. When its new master failed to act as all its training and instinct had taught it to expect, without moving any other part of its body, the dog slowly turned its head and looked at Brian with one ear cocked and on its face an expression of such utter bewilderment that the lad burst out in a shout of laughter he could not help

At the sharp burst of unexpected sound, from the cactus clump arose a covey of quail with a metallic whirring of wings. Instantly the dog crouched, as if to get out of line between the quail and the gun. And when the last quail disappeared into the depths of a ravine, and no shot had sounded the signal for the hunting dog to rush in and retrieve fallen game, that dusty, dilapidated, but still beautiful mongrel just sat down on its haunches and looked reproachfully at Brian. They would have to come to an understanding about this business at once. Then the dog could decide for itself whether this was the kind of master it wanted or did not want. Brian walked up to the dog. It beat its tail on the ground in a foolish, embarrassed way, still regarding the lad with amazement and reproach.

"No!" said Brian sternly. *"No!* You're a nice dog, and I'd like to have you for

my own, but if you come with me, you've got to learn that these quail and rabbits and other wild things are friends of mine too. Understand me? No! NO!"

The ears, erect for a moment, drooped disconsolately. So clearly was the dog questioning his motives that Brian found himself explaining them.

"It's lots more fun," said he, "just to be up here and to watch the wild things by day and the stars when it becomes night. I'll let you watch out for bobcats and coyotes, but you've got to leave the harmless things alone. I can't have you for a friend if you always want to kill my other friends."

Of course, the dog could not understand all, or perhaps any, of this. Besides, there was one thing that was just now even stronger than its recent fancy for Brian—and it was a thing the lad did not happen to think about. That dog was hungry! It had been accustomed to believe a hunt meant meat; yet instinct and training had taught it and its ancestors that game must not be eaten *alive or uncooked.* A human comrade was needed to cook what this dog would eat!

"You poor brute," said Brian, though still with a severe note. "I suppose you don't understand. But you've got to go. Go on, now! *Brrr-oo-oo!*"

Instead of retreating, the dog suddenly uttered a kind of heartbroken whine and came crawling and squirming to Brian's feet. There it laid its head on his shoe, let it rest there in absolute abasement for a few seconds, then raised its eyes to Brian's, opened its mouth and gave a long, mournful howl.

That was too much for Brian, who loved animals. In spite of himself—but, then, he *was* himself in the outdoors—he found himself suddenly down, his arms about that dusty, dilapidated mongrel's neck.

"Never mind, old fellow," he said huskily. "You just don't know any better. But you're a real dog, and I'm going to keep you and *teach* you better."

Presently he sprang to his feet, the inspiration of his new task filling him with elation.

"Come on!" he cried. "Camp's just over the brow of the hill. I won't say *brrr-oo-oo* anymore, unless I call you *Brr-oo-oo.* Why! That's your name— *Boru!* I'm Brian, and you're Brian Boru!"

They reached camp ten minutes later. Boru sat on his haunches and seemed to watch with a critical, experienced, but approving eye, the manner in which Brian arranged the stones for his campfire after clearing away all the adjacent dead leaves and twigs which might spread fire; and how he gathered firewood— small sticks of wood for the cook fire, and larger ones for the regular campfire;

finally, how this lad of the outdoors deftly made his blanket bed on level ground after picking out all the stones and sticks from the leaves that he scraped together for a mattress.

But the climax of their first day came when in the late dusk Brian lit his cook fire among the stones, got out his cook kit, and began to prepare his supper of beans, bacon, bread, and tea. Boru lay near the fire with his head resting on his forepaws, eyes following every movement of his young master, and nostrils twitching as the savory odor of frying bacon was wafted to them. Once he whined, and that was when Brian threw a piece of bacon rind into the fire as a precaution against attracting ants. Alas! Brian did not yet understand.

It was only in the middle of his supper, when he tossed to the dog a piece of bread soaked in bacon fat, and Boru sprang like a flash from a crouching position, snapped the morsel in midair, and swallowed it at one gulp, that Brian suddenly realized the agonies of self-denial this dog must have been undergoing for hours.

He stared at Boru, marveling at his own stupidity and thoughtlessness, marveling to think that this dog had not even attempted to take a bite of the unguarded bacon when its master's back was turned!

"You're certainly a great dog," said Brian, "and I believe you're going to teach me more than I can teach you. What's more, Boru, I've had half the supper. The rest is yours—except the chocolate, which I don't think you'd like."

Boru received his portion of supper with becoming modesty, but there was nothing modest in the way it was gulped down in about four swallows, including bacon, beans, and more bread soaked in grease. Then, after eating and drinking some water at the spring, he came over to where Brian was now stretched on his blankets with his arms under his head and his face upturned to the brightening stars. The dog crouched as near him as he could come without touching the blankets. His tail thumped a chant of joy and gratitude on the ground. Brian reached a hand from under his head and, still with his eyes on he stars, touched the dog's head and whispered contentedly: "Boru— Brian Boru!"

Inasmuch as Brian Borthwick was only fourteen years old, it may seem strange that he should be camping alone in the California hills. But thereby hangs a little tale in itself. With his father and mother, the boy lived about three miles south of the village of Laguna, with which there was a telephone connection. Laguna lies on the California coast about sixty miles south of Los Angeles.

The Borthwick house overlooked the blue Pacific, the coast highway running directly behind the house. In back of this road arose the Laguna hills which were the joy of Brian Borthwick's days.

His father, Neil Borthwick, had been a New York stockbroker and had suffered a breakdown in health. There was something wrong with one of his lungs, the doctors said, nothing serious if taken in time, as he and the doctors *did* take it. They prescribed a quiet life, plenty of outdoors, and freedom from business anxieties. It was Brian's father—his mother was at first dubious about it—who encouraged the lad in his instant liking for this new life away from a city.

"Let him get to love the open," said his father in answer to his mother's doubts. "Let him learn to be self-dependent. Besides . . ." he hesitated; they seldom spoke of the matter, "I want him to grow up a strong man before he tackles this modern business that strains one's health and often breaks it before one has achieved independence."

At first, when Brian spent whole days in the hills with his knapsack, his mother was anxious every moment until he returned. But as time went on, her fears gave way to a pleasure of anticipation of what new thing, or new story of adventure, he would bring back. One day he would see a bobcat skulking off. Another, he would report a prairie wolf, or coyote, which bolted as if it had seen a lion instead of a fourteen-year-old boy! As time went on, Brian, who was a studious observer, delighted his father and mother in the evenings by the open fireplace—for California nights are sometimes snappy—with a recital of his notes on things he had seen or reasoned for himself.

"But aren't you afraid—of the animals, Brian?" his mother would ask. "Wildcats—these coyotes—and I've heard there are still mountain lions."

"Mother," said Brian, "I've been thinking—and I believe I'm right—that no animals will hurt you if you do not seem to be trying to hurt them. In my book about wild things I read that even a rattlesnake is 'ordinarily an inoffensive creature.' "

His mother shuddered. Mr. Borthwick looked a little troubled.

"Don't experiment on that theory too much, son," said he. "If ever you see a rattlesnake, just you go the other way!"

But it was shortly after that, Brian's birthday coming around, that his mother presented him with a camper's first aid kit—a little metal box which, in its case, could be carried at the belt. Mr. Borthwick smiled over his wife's gift to their son, knowing full well the fears that prompted it. But Brian got as much joy out of it as some boys might have taken from the possession of a rifle. He was never tired of imagining what he would do with it in this or that emergency.

"Suppose I've burned my hand," he said to himself in his hill camp, with the little box open on his knees. "All right, here's the oil of salt phial. My eyes hurt from sun glare? A little boric acid in water. Got a thorn in my foot? Tweezers—right here! Then, after it is out, a touch from the iodine phial. Rattlesnake bites me? Keep cool. Make it bleed, even if you have to cut it a little with your own knife—and see that the knife's clean. Tie a handkerchief tourniquet to prevent bleeding and prevent poison from circulating, and sprinkle a little permanganate of potash—here's the phial all ready—on the bite. Then go home and call a doctor. But keep cool—always keep cool! Feel faint? Spirits of ammonia—right here in the second phial. Cut yourself? Wash it clean, touch with iodine, and bandage—here's the little gauze roll and the adhesive tape."

Brian chuckled with pride over his kit's efficiency, and a little over his own—in prospect. He found himself almost wishing that something would happen—nothing serious, you know; just a thorn, or a burned finger, or something like that—so he could doctor himself from this wonderful box.

By the end of his first year in the Laguna hills, Brian had become quite at home in the outdoors. He knew the times and the seasons of the wild things, furred, feathered, and leafy. In this self-education, his father found some relief from his worry over the necessity of cutting short the boy's high school courses when he fell ill and had to hasten with his family to this remote corner of the world.

It was some time before Brian's mother would consent to that first great adventure with the blankets in the hills overnight. She hugged Brian tightly when he came back the morning after the initial venture, thankful that he had neither caught cold nor been eaten up by a mountain lion. "Mother, it was wonderful!" the boy declared. "I didn't sleep a wink!"

"Didn't sleep a wink!" his mother echoed in dismay.

"I just couldn't! There was so much to see up there, and I hated to miss any of it!"

Then he went off in an animated description of the night—the stars, the faint rustle of wild animals in the brush, the flutter of roosting quail overhead in a tree, the smell of the leaves that were his bed, and the night air sweet with the aromatic scent of sagebrush.

Then the day arrived when Brian came home from the hills with a dog that made Mr. Borthwick stare and Mrs. Borthwick cry out in dismay. Not that there was anything about this dog to make anyone feel aversion. It was really a beautiful dog, with a coat immaculately white, except for some black and tan markings and several cuts and bruises which Brian had doctored with iodine from his precious kit, after treating Boru to a bath in the spring.

When Mr. Borthwick heard the story of that bath and the first use to which the birthday first aid kit had been put, he just sat down and laughed till his eyes were full of tears. But Mrs. Borthwick seemed rather troubled.

"Brian," she said, "I hate to have to disappoint you, but . . . you can't keep that dog, you know."

"Oh, Mother!" cried Brian, his face falling.

Mr. Borthwick stopped laughing at once and said, "No, son, you can't. It's too bad, too, because that's a first-rate hunter or I never saw one. And that's just it! Somebody is terribly worried over the loss of that dog, and that somebody will be back looking for him."

Brian sat all hunched up in an attitude of utter depression, but presently looked up with a brightening of hope.

"Suppose the owner doesn't come?" he asked.

"Mmm—well—we'll see," said Dad. "Only—until it's certain no one is likely to come and claim him, I wouldn't set my heart on that dog too much. It's not pleasant to become so attached to an animal that it almost breaks your heart when you lose him or to have to give him away. It's hard on the dog too. So we must not feed him or encourage him to stay around here."

So saying, he arose, went and opened the back door, and quietly invited Brian Boru to go out. The dog, after a glance at his young master, and getting no counterorder from him, obeyed. But once outside, he just looked back at the closed door, then walked over to the shade of an acacia tree, lay down, and fell asleep—with one eye half open on the door!

He was there when Brian went to bed that night after he had come out and condoled with Boru, and still there in the morning when he went out to see. The moment the sound of the opening door came to the dog's ears, he was alert. A second later with paws up on Brian's breast, he was barking a joyous "Good morning, trail mate!"

For days the dog remained around the house, being absent only for short periods during which he presumably hunted for food elsewhere. The fact that he received no such encouragement, as yet, around the Borthwick house, did not seem to affect his allegiance to Brian in the least. But as a rule, if the lad were in the house, Boru was under the acacia tree, awaiting his appearance. If Brian left the house, even stealing out by an unseen door, the strange instinct of the dog, or his sense of smell, informed him instantly, and he'd dash to that particular door. The remarkable thing is that he did not bestir himself if *anyone else* opened an unseen door. Boru's nose told him in advance that this was not the object of his adoration.

"Greater love hath no dog than this—" Mr. Borthwick laughingly said one day. Then he stopped as the rest of the paraphrased saying occurred to him. "It might, at that!" he muttered, staring at Brian's mother, who suddenly became very pale.

"Neil," she whispered, "what did you mean by that?"

"Oh, nothing, nothing," he said hastily.

"Then," said Brian's mother, "I hope, whoever owns it never comes!"

But that there was great likelihood of his coming was apparent when, a few days later, Dr. Bransom arrived from Laguna on a periodic visit to Mr. Borthwick. Brian had just started into the hills with his outfit, and, of course, Boru had immediately attached himself. The boy could hardly remain a prisoner in his home because of a dog.

"Just passed Brian with a fine pup," said the doctor, who was a bit of a sportsman himself. "Looked like a mighty hunter himself, all loaded for camp and a bear—except for a gun. Where'd he pick up the huntin' dog?"

They told him the story of Brian and Brian Boru. The doctor seemed to be puzzling over something.

"Interesting," said he, "but it seems to me I've seen that dog before. He's something of a tramp if he's the same animal. It's in my head, somehow, that Falkner, a small rancher up Laguna Canyon, owns him—if anybody does."

"Sorry to hear that," said Neil Borthwick. "Do you think this Faulkner would sell him? Try and find out for me, doctor, if he really owns Boru, and if he does, see if he can be induced to part with him. Tell him he might as well, for locks, bolts, and bars can't keep Brian and Brian Boru apart.

"A week ago," he went on, laughing, "we locked Boru in the garage while Brian went into the hills. We wanted to see if we could break the dog of the habit of following. But he overtook Brian before the lad got to his camp in the hills."

"How did he get out?" asked the doctor.

"When he found he couldn't eat through the wall he went headlong through the window. Anyway, we found the window smashed, and Brian used up all his iodine on Boru, who was a bit cut with broken glass."

"Huh!" chuckled the doctor. "Some dog! Some boy! Sort of till-death-do-us partnership—hullo! What's the trouble?" Dr. Bransom suddenly broke off, his eyes sharply fixed on Mrs. Borthwick, who had sunk into a chair, her head drooping oddly to one side.

"Quick, Borthwick—some cold water and a towel! Your wife has fainted!"

It may have been the doctor's suggestion of a partnership ending in tragedy or it may have been that mother instinct which is sometimes almost second sight, or it may have been mere coincidence. But, as a matter of fact, the thing happened just about the time Brian's mother had that fainting spell, from which she quickly recovered and felt foolish.

It was on the trip back from the camp just over the ridge of the hills. Brian was swinging along whistling happily as he followed the dim trail which his own feet had made through sagebrush, around cactus clumps, down into and up out of ravines, always working toward a grove of eucalyptus trees where an old wagon road led to the coast highway and the house overlooking the Pacific.

At the particular moment he had just emerged from some brushy substance going into open ground where the sunlight played all day. Boru was then several yards behind him on the right, the dog having stopped to investigate some stray scent its nose had encountered. But as Brian quickened his steps and said, "Come on, Boru!" the dog hurried to come up with him. Then it happened—so rapidly that Brian hardly realized *what* was happening—what *had* happened until it was practically over.

He saw nothing out of the common. But Boru did. There was no time to stop and "point." The thing was not four feet in front of Brian. Two more steps and he, quite unaware of what was there, would have stepped on it.

The curious thing—as Brian reflected afterward—was that it made no sound. But—as Brian also reflected afterward—you could not blame a wild creature for giving no warning when, awakened from a pleasant sleep in the sun, it found it was too late to retreat. And there *are* times when this particular menace attacks without warning, especially when it is sleepy.

But the keen eyes of the hunting dog had seen the slight movement of the thing as it stirred from sleep. Boru knew what that movement meant—what it portended for the master. The dog made no sound, either, save a low, harsh snarl as it launched itself headlong upon the thing.

Even then Brian's eyes did not quite comprehend what they saw, which was simply a tangle of dog and—something else. And just as Boru came to the ground at the end of that tigerlike spring, the lad heard the dog's jaws snap together with the sound of a sprung trap.

Then came another sound—one he had never heard before in his life. It came from the tangle of dog and the thing at which Boru had launched himself. The sound was a harsh rustling, yet not unlike the nerve-racking hiss of a leaky faucet. Almost instantly the sound ceased, and a long reddish "stick," which Brian had indifferently noted on his path, suddenly became animated and flexible and wound itself around Boru's body. Instantly Brian Borthwick knew what that reddish "stick" was—a red diamondback rattlesnake—the most dangerous, perhaps, of all the *Crotalus* family, and its body was as thick as Brian's own arm at the elbow!

Realization came to him in a flash, even as the happening itself came and was over in the space of perhaps two flashes. The first of these flashes was when Boru sprang and snapped his jaws. But a rattlesnake is swift—swifter even than a hunting dog. Boru's jaws closed over nothing, making that sprung-trap sound as his teeth clashed together. The second flash was like a double bolt of lightning—Boru and the snake in action at the same time. Again Boru snapped at the reptile whose full five-foot length the dog's paws vainly tried to pin to earth. At the same time, the rattlesnake, its head and neck free for the moment, struck with its fangs at the dog.

Both scored—and the battle was over. Boru's jaws had closed over the serpent's body, breaking the easily dislocated spinal column. Simultaneously the rattlesnake had buried its fangs in the fleshy upper part of Boru's left hind leg, at which he uttered a yelp of pain and sprang back, tearing his own flesh from the hooked fangs of the snake. The latter remained where it had been, squirming helplessly, as good as dead for all the harm it would ever do again. But Brian had no eyes for the snake. He had *seen the finish* of that fight and how Boru sprang away with two spots spreading on his white coat like red ink on blotting paper.

The emergency had come! For a moment Brian was too shocked by the horror of the thing to have complete control of his wits. But almost at once he pulled himself together. One glance told him that the rattlesnake was, and would remain, helpless. It could make no further trouble—would die presently. Another glance showed that Boru was not greatly concerned—apparently! The dog was sitting on his haunches, head twisted around, and was rapidly licking the punctures made by the two fangs.

Quickly Brian tore off his belt with his hunting knife and first aid kit on it. From its sheath he whipped out the keen blade and rushed to Boru's side, intending to make a cut across the fang punctures so that the wound would bleed more freely.

"Boru! Boru!" he gasped. "I've got to hurt you—but don't you mind! You know I wouldn't hurt you, unless—let me get at it, Boru! Let me—"

To his amazement and consternation, the dog ceased licking the snakebite for just a second, looked up into Brian's eyes, its own usually affectionate ones shot with ferocity, and its lips curled back from its teeth. And Brian Boru *snarled* at his beloved young master! A sickening chill struck Brian's heart. Already, he believed, the deadly venom was at work, had touched Boru's brain. The dog was going mad! But even at the risk of being bitten, he had to do something.

"Boru!" he cried sharply. "How dare you snarl at me! I'm going to cut that bite, even if—"

As he was speaking he had seized Boru by the scruff of the neck and pulled his head away from the wound his tongue was washing. Instantly the dog, with a snarl that was a final, ominous warning, jerked his head free, closed his jaws over Brian's wrist and, without sinking his teeth, kept the wrist in that viselike grip, as if to say, "I do not wish to bite you, master, but I *must* if you *will* interfere with what I am doing!"

But Brian did not understand. Only he said in a broken kind of way: "Let go, Boru—let go!"

With a whine the dog obeyed and at once fell to licking the wound again. Only this time, after a few more licks, he began to chew the snake bite with the curious suction of a dog trying to remove a burr from his hide. And as he chewed, blood began to flow freely from the wound.

"Don't do that, Boru!" pleaded Brian. "I can do it better. Let me—"

Again he had tried to assist the dog. This time Boru snapped at his hand, but missed—whether by accident or intent there is no saying. Anyway, at that vicious click of canine teeth within an inch of his hand, Brian knew it was no use.

"What am I to do?" he cried. "He won't let me help!"

For nearly a minute, he sat there, thinking that this was the end of their happy comradeship! He found himself wondering if it would be better to knock Boru senseless and then administer proper treatment than to sit there and watch the dog die in agony. Yes—he would do it—with a rock if he had to! It was the only way. And then he would work hard to give Boru a chance to recover and live on.

He sprang to his feet and looked about him. Indifferently he noted that the rattlesnake was still squirming, but less violently. He picked up the nearest large stone and put the venomous creature out of pain. Then, with the same stone—and his heart sick for what he had to do—he was about to turn to Boru.

But just then he heard a plaintive whine at his heels and felt a soft nuzzle nosing his ankles. He looked down. Boru was there at his feet. And there at his feet Boru lay down, again with that plaintive whine, and seemed as if about to curl up and go to sleep.

The chunk of rock fell from Brian's hand. Something told him there was no longer any need for that stone or that it would not help. Boru was again quite docile, perhaps because he was weak—dying—or possibly because there was nothing further to be done, the dog having done nearly all that could be done.

But Brian did not think all that was necessary *had* been done. True, the big red blot on the dog's thigh told him the bleeding had been attended to, and the dog had doubtless sucked a good deal of the poison from the immediate wound. He would not have to cut, thank goodness, but he must put the stuff from the phial into that wound. That stuff would pass into the dog's veins, and it was the antidote for this particular venom.

Out of the first aid kit he took the little phial of shiny black stuff and uncorked it. Boru seemed stupefied. He only lifted his head and whined faintly as his master dropped the tiny coal dustlike crystals into the wound. Then, as the permanganate of potash stung the raw place, Boru yelped and again attempted to chew at the wound which the chemical had now stained an ugly purple. But Brian held the dog's head back, and Boru, making no further show of biting, surrendered to the boy's mastership with only a dubious howl of uncertainty as to the wisdom of it.

Then, as if resigned to whatever might now come, Boru curled up and seemed to go asleep. Presently Brian thought the dog was dead—or dying. But then he noticed Boru's breathing. He was not panting, but breathing steadily, although a little rapidly. The fight for life was on!

After he had tied a handkerchief tightly around the dog's thigh above the wound, there was no more Brian could do, except—what was that rule? Oh, yes. Keep cool. Go home. Get a doctor. But always keep cool! Five minutes later, with a limp, but again conscious, dog in his arms—a dog which occasionally tried to lick his face—Brian Borthwick was hastening down the trail to the house.

Mr. and Mrs. Borthwick were in the living room, for outside the sun was glary and quite hot, and Brian's mother was still a little weak from that curious fainting spell. Into the room suddenly burst their son. Brian's face was white, and in his arms was a limp dog which was no lightweight to carry.

"What the dickens—" began Mr. Borthwick.

"Quick, Dad! Get a doctor!" gasped the breathless and almost exhausted boy. "Boru's been bitten by a rattlesnake!"

"Bitten by a rattlesnake!" Brian's mother screamed. "Put it down—at once—outside! It may go mad and snap at you! Oh, I knew something was happening!"

"Hold on, Mary—" began Mr. Borthwick soothingly. But Brian burst in with a kind of angry protest.

"He can bite me if he likes! He's entitled to do it, for he took the bite of the rattlesnake to save *me*!"

There was an instant of terrible stillness in that room. Mrs. Borthwick was staring, her face pallid and twitching curiously. Then Brian's father sprang to the telephone and called Dr. Bransom.

At the same time, Mrs. Borthwick, controlling her nerves, did an odd but very womanly thing. She quietly opened her own bedroom door, pulled down the coverlet of the bed, and said to the boy with the wilting dog in his arms, "Lay him here, Brian. He shall have my own bed. And if he gets well we'll never, *never* let him leave us."

When Dr. Bransom arrived he looked curiously at his first dog patient and placed a hand over Boru's irregularly beating heart while Brian poured out the whole story.

"Some dog!" muttered the doctor as he dissolved the broken-off half of a small white tablet in the barrel of a hypodermic syringe.

"There's little I can do," said he, "that Brian and the dog himself haven't done already. All I *know* to do—not being a dog doctor—is to steady and strengthen his heart with a little strychnia."

Boru winced as the needle punctured his skin. But Brian was holding his head while whispering assurance that it was all right. Boru probably believed it was, because five minutes later, that glorious mongrel had dropped off into a natural sleep, which lasted until evening. Then, finding that the beloved scent had moved—that is, Brian had gone for a much needed supper—Boru astonished everybody by trotting into the dining room and wrinkling an inquiring nose in the direction of some savory odors of food!

When Dr. Bransom looked in again in the evening to see how his "patient" was coming along, he found the Borthwick family ranged in a pretty picture about the open fire—for even in the late spring the evenings are cool. Mrs. Borthwick was at one side of the hearth, sewing; her husband at the other, reading. On the rug, with his hands cupping his chin and his eyes fixed upon the glowing eucalyptus logs, was Brian. Beside him, with nose just touching his body, was Brian Boru.

"Can you beat that?" said the doctor, staring at a dog that seemed to be quite well again. "I've heard of it, but never quite believed it till now."

"Believed what, doctor?" asked Mr. Borthwick.

"That generations of hunting dogs out West here have been bitten so often by rattlesnakes that a certain amount of immunity develops in the strain. That fact, together with its instinctive first aid to itself, and Brian's medicine kit, saved that dog's life."

"After it had saved my boy's," said Mrs. Borthwick, bending forward and touching Boru's head with a great tenderness of love and gratitude. "I don't care who the owner is, doctor; he will never get Boru away from this family."

"How about it, doctor?" asked Mr. Borthwick, still anxious on that point. "Did you find out about the rancher in the canyon?"

"Yes," replied the doctor. "It's his dog—Falkner's—of the Three-Spring Ranch up Laguna Canyon. He tells me this dog wouldn't stay home—always wanted to go hunting. When Falkner let a week go by without a gunning trip, the dog would just go off hunting on its own account or pick up with any stranger who came along smelling of sagebrush!"

Brian's heart went heavy on the instant. So a man named Falkner owned Boru, and this man lived only a few miles away!

"Too bad if Brian has to give him up after *this*—and breaking him of the killing habit too," said Neil Borthwick gloomily.

"Oh, but he doesn't have to give him up!" chuckled the doctor. "I was talking with Falkner just this evening. Told him the story of the boy and the dog and the rattlesnake, and Falkner, who's a good sort, came right back at me: 'You tell this Brian Borthwick for me that he owes a lot to that dog,' he says, 'and if ever I hear he isn't treating the pup as it deserves I'll come and take it back! Otherwise,' he says, 'it's his dog from now on—and God bless 'em both!' "

For a few minutes Brian believed that he had not heard aright. Then realization dawned. Tears started in his eyes, and he buried his face on the neck of a dog that at once made wild efforts to lick his face.

Boru's tail beating joyously on the floor was the only thing that broke a stillness during which three grown-ups suddenly found that they were blinking back tears themselves.

And when, for the first time, the dog was allowed that night to sleep on a little bed of burlap and an old coat in a corner of Brian's room, Mrs. Borthwick kissed the glorious mongrel on its cold muzzle, and Neil Borthwick, laying a hand on its head, said, "Good night, Brian Boru *Borthwick!*"

* * * * *

"Brian Boru," by Stephen Chalmers. Published August 1928 in St. Nicholas. *If anyone has information regarding the author's next of kin, please send the information to Joe Wheeler (P.O. Box 1246, Conifer, CO 80433). Stephen Chalmers (1880–1935) was born in Dunoon, Scotland, and wrote poetry and many short stories and novels.*

The Stork That Was Late

Charles David Stewart

Over a hundred years ago, this story was written. Communicationwise, it was a different world then.

In that bygone world, an aging stork making its last migrational trip home to Holland—handicapped though it was by two lame legs—could, by enduring, change the destiny of an old couple about to lose their beloved home.

* * * * *

In the city of Rotterdam, in Holland, there stands in the middle of an arched bridge over the public canal a black statue. It was once a good likeness of a famous man named Erasmus. But in the course of time the countenance slowly changed—so slowly that the busy market folk, who clattered across the bridge with their dogcarts laden with milk and vegetables, did not notice that the statue grew less like Erasmus every day.

One morning an old burgher of the town stopped on his way across the bridge to inspect the statue, which he had not closely observed since he gave his final approval of it on the day it was erected. He opened his small eyes wide, and his grave and stolid expression changed to one of wonder and amazement. Then he hurried away as fast as his short legs would carry him to the public gallery where the picture of Erasmus was. When he realized that

his eyes had not deceived him, he hurried back to the statue, and stood before it, more perplexed than ever. Erasmus had surely changed.

Now, if the old burgher had not noticed this, the story I am going to tell about Dederick Schimmelpennick and his good wife, and the stork Peyster, would never have been told.

One evening, about a year after this happened, old Dederick Schimmelpennick and his good wife sat in the doorway of their house, looking at the statue of Erasmus in the distance. Dederick held his wife's hand in his, for they were in great trouble. For many years it had been their custom to sit thus and look at the statue of Erasmus as it shone brightly in the sunset. And why should they not look with pride upon the shining statue, for was it not Dederick who had kept it bright these many years? But this evening, and for many evenings past, the statue did not gleam with the luster that had lent brightness to their lives. It had grown to look darker and darker in the sunset, and the hopes of Dederick and his wife had grown darker day by day since it was discovered that the frequent scouring of the statue had changed Erasmus—eyes, nose, and ears. And at last their life was as dark as the statue itself, for their little savings were almost exhausted, and Dederick was old.

Dederick pressed his wife's hand, and they sat thinking in silence, for they had been talking about their only son, who had sailed away many years ago to try his fortune in the world.

"If Peter should ever return," said the wife, "I know that as he comes up the canal and sees Erasmus looking so dark, he will think that we are dead. I wonder if we shall ever see him again?"

"I doubt not," said Dederick, "that some day, when he has made his fortune, he will return and be the comfort of our old age. But alas! He does not know that I am no more allowed to scour Erasmus and earn the daily bread."

"Yes," answered the good wife, "if Peter knew that, he would come to us now, for he was a dutiful son. But he must come soon or it will be too late. Before another month has passed our last guilder will be gone, and I fear we shall have to leave the house."

"Yes," said Dederick, "already the storks are returning from the south, and the time when we shall have no home is near at hand. Today I looked up at the chimney top to see if Peyster had arrived, but the nest is still empty."

"I fear," said Mistress Schimmelpennick, "that Peyster is too old to make the long flight again. Last year he was almost exhausted. Do you not remember, Dederick, that when we saw him coming, the young stork supported him on his back and helped him along?"

"Yes, I remember it," said Dederick. "And do you not remember that when old Peyster was young he helped his mother back after his first flight and put her in the same nest in which she had raised and tended him the year before?"

"And do you remember, Dederick, how our little Peter said, 'Mother, when I am able to go out into the world, I will be like Peyster and support you when you are old and weak'?"

"I do," said Dederick, wiping his eyes with the back of his hand. "Peter is a dutiful son, for he is a true Dutch boy. And is it not the Dutch who shelter the stork on their rooftree, and hold him in reverence because of his care for the older birds? But I fear that old Peyster, like us, is almost beyond help. Last year his lame leg was very weak. And if Peter does not come soon neither old Peyster nor we will be here to greet him."

In the middle of February all the storks came flying back from Egypt and Palestine and the plains of North Africa and occupied once more their nests on the rooftrees and chimney tops of Holland. But still the nest on the Schimmelpennicks' chimney top was empty. There were still no tidings of Peter, and the hopes of the aged couple were almost gone.

"I cannot understand," said Dederick, "why the young stork does not come to the nest. Maybe he has been delayed in helping old Peyster, and we shall yet see them both. For does not the good book say, 'The stork in the heavens hath its appointed times'?"

As old Dederick had no work to do, he sat by the window and watched the storks arriving from the south. He waited three long days after the time that Peyster had always returned; and although no more storks were to be seen in the sky, he still kept watch.

On the fourth day Dederick cried, "Look, look!" and his good wife hurried to the window.

"It must be they," said she.

The two birds were flying slowly, and now and then one of them darted under the other and supported it in its flight.

"I know it is Peyster," said Dederick. "See how his leg hangs down."

Sure enough, it was Peyster and the young stork. They lowered their flight toward the nest, and Dederick and his wife ran out into the yard. As the young stork left Peyster to fly alone, Peyster wavered in the air. As he gathered in his wings and settled on the edge of the roof, with one leg he struggled to keep his footing, and flapped his wings wildly—then fell to the ground.

"What is this?" exclaimed Dederick, as he took Peyster's leg and examined it tenderly.

"Poor old Peyster, there is something the matter with his other leg," said Mistress Schimmelpennick. Somebody had evidently been caring for Peyster, for his leg was carefully bound up in red silk.

When Dederick loosened the threads and began to unwind the bandage, his nervous fingers could hardly work fast enough. He discovered that he had in his hands the silk handkerchief which the mother had tied around Peter's neck when he left them to go on the ship. But what was his surprise, when he had the handkerchief loose, to find his hands full of banknotes, and with them a letter. He was so amazed that he held his hands in front of him and stood looking at them, stock-still. For a moment he did not move any more than if he had been the statue of Erasmus set up in his own yard.

You may be sure it did not take Mrs. Schimmelpennick long to bring Dederick his spectacles, and this is what Dederick read aloud to his wife:

My Dear Father and Mother:

I send you my love. Since you heard from me last I have visited many strange lands. I have not been able to write to you for the reason that in the part of Africa where I have been I had no opportunity to send mail to Holland. I have just arrived in Egypt, and as soon as I can settle my affairs here I will come home and start in business in old Rotterdam, for I have been very prosperous. I have often wished that you could share my good fortune. One day shortly after I arrived here, I sat watching the storks, and thinking how soon many of them would be in my fatherland, for it was the season for them to fly. What was my surprise to see old Peyster standing on one leg on the bank of the river, where he had been catching frogs. I knew him by the way his lame leg hung down. He had his head tucked between his shoulders, taking a nap, and was resting, I imagined, for the long flight he had in mind. I believe I should have known Peyster even had he never been lame. When you get this you will know what came into my mind the minute I saw dear old Peyster. And now, my dear father, you must give up your work of keeping the statue clean, for by the time this money is used I shall be home to care for you. For a long time I have been worried with the thought that you were too aged for such dangerous employment. I am sure this will reach you, and I thank God that He has given me the means of relieving you at once.

Your dutiful son, Peter.

* * * * *

"The Stork That Was Late," by Charles David Stewart. Published October 1900 in St. Nicholas. *Charles David Stewart, a native of Zanesville, Ohio, wrote prolifically during the first half of the twentieth century.*

FLAPJACK

Carter Hamilton

He was just a forlorn, little lost puppy who was looking for a home. He found it!
But then came Silver Tip—twice!

* * * * *

He turned one clean half somersault from nowhere and landed plunk on his back at my feet. I said, "Flapjacks!" That's how he got his name. He was only an Indian's cur, the forlornest little waif of a lost puppy, with the most beautiful dogs' eyes I have ever seen. He scrambled to his feet and used his eyes—that settled it for us. Without further introduction, we offered him the remains of our dinner. He accepted it with three gulps and then stood wagging his poor little tail, asking for more.

We were camping and trailing out in the Wind River Mountains— Brandt and I—back of the Shoshone Indian Reservation, and we had halted for dinner in a small cañon in the shade of the rock wall from whose summit Flapjack had tried his little acrobatic stunt. Whether he came from an Indian encampment nearby, which we had not seen, or was just plain lost and fending for himself alone in the wilderness, we did not know. He told us about fending for one's self while he ate his dinner, an' that it was "an *awful*" hard

life and sometimes "*very* discouraging." After dinner he told us that our scraps were the very best food he had ever eaten; that our outfit, our horses and mule, the finest he had ever seen; that we ourselves were gods, wise and very great; that he loved the ground we trod on, and only asked to stay with us forever. So he stayed.

Jinny, the mule, returned his compliments unopened and told him what she thought of him by shoving the underside of her off hind hoof and putting back her ears. But then, Jinny was the only aristocratic person in camp, in her own opinion, and you may take that for what it is worth. She didn't prejudice us against Flapjack. Still, Brandt and I happened not to share Jinny's opinion of herself. Brandt was in the habit of remarking on seventeen separate and several occasions each day that "even fer a mule, Jinny is the low downdest one I ever set eyes on."

At the sight of her hoof, Flapjack made a ludicrous little duck with his head and came back to us, volubly explaining that, "Of course, the mule being *yours,* don't you know? She simply must be the very finest, sweetest-tempered animal in the world, don't you know? And altogether above reproach, don't you know?" That won us completely.

And he never once reproached her for anything she did—even when she kicked him into the river. He treated her with distant courtesy always, without so much as a *yap* in her direction. And it wasn't because he was afraid of mules, either—Brandt and I will deny that imputation against his valor to our dying day. Let a strange mule or horse get in among ours, and Flapjack was a very lion of ferocity until he had *yapped* him out of sight.

"Think we'd better look for their camp?" I asked, putting the dishes into Jinny's pack.

"What, the pup's Indians? Not *much!*" answered Brandt. "If they haven't seen us, let 'em alone. An' if they have—why, we've got to wait proper introductions. I move we *hike.*"

So we hiked, and Flapjack hiked with us.

We kept on our trail, if such it could be called: a trail which probably no white man but ourselves had ever set foot upon. We were bound for a little lake that we knew, crammed with the most innocent fish on earth. No, I am not going to tell you where. There are some things you must find out for yourself, if you are game for it, just as we did; otherwise, you don't deserve to know.

After some ten days we arrived, without either adventure or misadventure, at our happy fishing ground, and made camp on a little precipice at whose foot a deep, dark pool lured monster and luscious rarities.

In spite of his hard journey, little Flapjack had improved amazingly as to health, not as to manners, for from the first day we knew him, he had better manners than any other dog I ever met. If you flung him a crust, he so appreciated it—it was the very nicest crust, the daintiest morsel, one could have; just as everything we did was simply perfect in his eyes. And he wasn't servile about it, either. He simply *approved* of everything we did, and told us so in an eloquent, voiceless way of his own.

We made camp for a two weeks' stay, felled a tree for a backlog, and fixed things generally to be comfortable, all under his supervising eye. And when it was done, and the friendship fire lighted, he lay down before it as one of us and said, "This is *home.*"

So we fished and were happy, and we fished some more and were happier, and we fished more and more and were happier and happier every day. Do you understand the feeling? If you have known Wyoming campfires, you do.

Sometimes we tramped to distant shores of the lake, "so's not to git our own fish too eddicated," Brandt explained, though generally we fished at our camp from a fallen forest monarch lying out over our deep hole. We used much craft and almost any kind of bait, and drew up monsters I do not dare to describe in cold print. Brandt used to say, "Them fish is so blame' innercent, y' could ketch um with a shoe button on a buttonhook, if y' had it handy"—which I didn't. And thus we lived one blessed week of glorious days between heavenly sleeps—that is, until the day of the great catch.

"Somethin' comin'," said Brandt one day, as he looked at the great catch laid in a row in front of our tent.

"Supper!" I yelled.

"I don't mean that. I mean *somethin*'," replied Brandt, meditatively. "Jever notice that whenever y' strike the great catch somethin' comes right bang top of it to take y' down? Every time an' *every* time it's so. That's what I mean. I bet it's Indians—seem to sense it that way—Indians."

"I seem to sense it that we've got to clean those fish before it gets dark *and* fry them *and* eat them," I said. "Do we pack the water up or the fish down?"

"Water up, I guess," said Brandt, proudly looking on the great catch. "A blame' sight less to pack, er I'm a sinner. Hang um on a string an' souse um off the log after."

So Brandt with one canvas bucket and the agate kettle, and I with the other bucket and the coffeepot, meandered down our little trail to the water's edge, and dipped our household supply. We were gone, all told, twenty minutes. Brandt was in the lead, Flapjack at my heel, for he superintended all the camp operations, mealtime being his great opportunity.

There were two high rock steps at the end of our path that brought us up to our level. Flapjack ran around through the brush by a trail of his own to meet us at the top. Brandt stepped over; I followed.

"Jumpin' giraffes!" Brandt exclaimed.

At that instant I saw our last fish disappear into a great red mouth in one end of a brush pile, and the mouth said, *"Woof!"*

At the word Brandt's canvas bucket hurtled through the air and landed *quush!* on a big, "silver tip" grizzly's nose.

The grizzly said, *"Woofsh-spshpts!"* very loud.

The bucket was Flapjack's cue to go on with his part, and he did. He went after the bucket with a wild *Yee-ap!* and a flying leap, and landed somewhere in the neighborhood of the spot just vacated by the bucket.

The grizzly emitted something between a shriek and a groan, bounded up like a rubber ball, cleared the top level at one jump, and disappeared into the brush, squealing, with Flapjack *yee-ap-yapping* at his heels!

We heard the bushes crackle and crash while old Silver Tip ran and squealed. We heard little Flapjack *yee-ap-yapping* his views on bear in general and big ones in particular. The echoes ceased, and the sounds grew fainter and fainter and fainter, and we were swallowed up by the great silences.

"Well, I never!" groaned Brandt at last, looking ruefully at the revolver in his hand. "*Such* a chance spoilt by a pup—a plain, stump-tail Indian pup!"

"Plucky, though, wasn't it?"

"Plucky! If y' call it plucky to run after a thing when y' don't know what it is an' jest throw yerself at its head till y' find out! But he won out, all the same!" added Brandt. "Yes, siree, he *won out*—on sheer pluck! What'd I tell y'? 'Twasn't Indians, but it sure was something—the whole catch o' fish is gone—and our supper."

"I'm thinking of Flapjack," I said. " 'Fraid he's done for by this, poor little fellow."

"Oh, he'll be back to supper," replied Brandt, confidently; and an hour later, tongue lolling, tail erect, Flapjack sauntered into camp.

Proud of himself? Well, rather! So were we, and we told him so. He went from one to the other of us, offering his congratulations on our having such a speedy dog in camp with us. "Bears? Pooh! What are grizzly bears? You don't have to be such a very brave dog to drive *them* off! Pooh! Do it again any time you say!"—that sort of talk, you know. For a few minutes we were just a bit afraid he was looking down on us for a couple of softies—*we* hadn't jumped at a grizzly and boxed its ears! But no, he was much too fine a gentleman for that. We had fed him when he was hungry, and we were just as good as he was—oh, every whit!—even if we hadn't driven old Silver Tip across the landscape squealing like a pig! He made us feel perfectly at ease with him, and when suppertime came he quietly laid aside his glory with a "let's forget it" air and ate with us like an equal and the campfire brother that he was.

"Silver Tip'll be back tomorrow," I remarked.

"Nope," replied Brandt. "Don't you guess it. This time tomorrow mornin' he'll strike Yallastone Park, an' this time tomorrow night he'll be over in Montana visitin' his aunt in the country. If y' want *him* you'll have to take an express train; an' y' won't ketch him then. He'll hike over three states 'fore he stops. I know bears—they ain't coyotes. Flappie, what d' ye think about it?"

Flapjack replied that he agreed with Brandt absolutely, that he, too, knew bears "tremenjous well," and he did a great deal of tail wagging to prove it.

So I took their word for it—two against one—and silently pondered the great event. For it was an event to me at that time—my first sight of Silver Tip in his native wilderness. Those were the early days of Wyoming campfires for me, and I had then seen very little of the larger game.

But even though two against one, they were wrong, and in this wise it all happened five days later.

We had gone to our second pool three miles upshore, and had made a good catch—mine was very good. It was my turn to do chores, and Brandt was after "one great whale." I have noticed that Brandt always is after "one great whale" whenever my catch is better than his. So he stayed out, and I went back to camp, personally conducted by Flapjack, a string of lesser whales in my hand.

And I almost ran into Silver Tip before I saw him—for Silver Tip was in the tent! He had already munched the camera and a few other trifles of like sort and was at the moment supping on my last film (all the views of the trip!), which hung out of his mouth and curled about like a live ribbon while he clawed it.

Silver Tip said, *"Wo-o-of!"* and struck out with his paw—at the film, probably, though I thought he was striking at me. Anyhow, he struck out—I saw that. I struck out with the fish in my hand, and hit him *swat* on the side of the head! That started it—he knew what I was.

I dropped the fish I was carrying and jumped, pulling my six-shooter. With one bound he was out of the tent after me. The next instant I found myself playing hide-and-seek with him around a big tree, to the tune of *Woof-woof* and of *Yap-yap-yap-yee-ap* from Flapjack.

I am not sure but at this stage of the game Silver Tip thought he was as much pursued as pursuing, and that if I had given him time and a fair chance, he would have changed his mind about me and decided I wasn't worth it. But I didn't. Something kept saying in my ear, *Shoot! Shoot!*

I had a dim sort of realization that I couldn't shoot over my head or behind my back or under my feet, and take flying leaps at the same time about a tree. So I bolted for the next tree, meaning to turn there and shoot. As I did so, Flapjack dashed from behind Bruin and nipped him in the flank. That distraction gave me one extra second and my chance. I fired and struck him amidships. Bruin turned and snapped viciously at his wound. On that, Flapjack nipped his ear. I fired a second time, but only grazed him.

He rushed me then so that I bolted to the next tree, then across the open space to the third. I gained time by this; I knew what I was going to do, and Bruin didn't. I say time—it was probably three seconds. As he came at me, Flapjack dashed back and forth between us, yapping and pirouetting just out of reach. Bruin felt annoyed, dropped me to settle Flapjack, and I fired my third shot. It ripped along his muzzle and bedded itself in his jaw. The roar he gave frightened me so that it literally fired my revolver! That bullet became part of the landscape.

Two shots more! flashed across my mind. *And two more such shots and it's puss in the corner till I die.*

Bruin was crazy now with rage and pain. Self-control was not one of his virtues. For two seconds Flapjack held the field. I repeated my triangle trick in that two seconds, and with a quick start, ran between two trees, bolted for the open and turned.

But I had miscalculated the bear's distance or his speed. As I turned to shoot, he rose to his feet almost over me, a mountain of sudden death.

And then little Flapjack did his great act—took one wild, flying leap plump into Bruin's chest and fell flat on his own back. He recovered in a second—but a second too late. The mountain dropped on all fours; a huge paw swung out, and little Flapjack went through the air like a shuttlecock.

That one second saved my life. The bear, with head down, faced me. I fired. The shot took him clean between the eyes. His great hulk lurched forward and literally fell on my feet.

I have no idea how long I stood there afterward, stock-still, turned to stone. I seemed to be waiting for Flapjack to do his act again—take a flying leap and sing, *"Yee-ap-yap!"* I listened and listened for *yee-ap-yap,* but heard only a muffled *thud, thud, thud, thud*—my own heart. I wondered why, and why, and *why* he didn't come to congratulate me on the victory—*our* victory. Around me lay the soft silence of the forest, at my feet the huge prowler that had just met death.

Then, on a sudden, I heard a piteous little moan, and I came to myself—and I understood everything.

I found him at the foot of a giant pine, twenty feet away.

I fell on my knees beside him.

"Flapjack, little dog!" I cried out.

And his beautiful, pain-filled eyes looked into mine and said, "If you're all right, that's all I care for!" and his little tongue feebly lapped my hand.

"Oh, dear little dog," I said, "you have given your life for mine. Bravest, truest heart in all the world! You saved your friend; do you know it? You won out!"

He tried to rise, but he was past rising ever again.

"Goodbye, brave heart!" I said.

* * * * *

If someday you should find a promontory by a lonely Wyoming lake, find a giant pine tree and a pile of stone beneath, find on the great trunk a smooth-cut slab, and read the burnt-in letters:

FLAPJACK Aug. 9, 1897,

don't laugh, please; you'll know what it means.

* * * * *

"Flapjack," by Carter Hamilton. Published January 1906 in St. Nicholas. *Carter Hamilton wrote for popular magazines around the turn of the twentieth century.*

THROUGH THE STORM

Mary Woodbury Caswell

What could be worse than being lost in the midst of a howling blizzard? And a wrong turn would most likely cost her her life.
Enter the most unlikely rescuer!

* * * * *

A boy and girl, Jack and Kathleen Markham, were swinging along on snowshoes over the sparkling floor of a northwestern prairie. The thin crust on the snow was hard enough to reduce the labor of snowshoeing to a minimum, and the biting air flushed their faces, of which the likeness sufficiently proclaimed their relationship without the brotherly frankness of the boy's comment: "Look out, Kathleen! Slow up a little; you're a great traveler all right, but no girl, or boy either, can strike that gait and keep it up for long."

The girl smiled as she reduced her speed and then bent to look at a faint track on the crust.

"There's your coyote, Jack," she said. "The middle toe is gone."

"Miserable little brute!" was his wrathful response. "I might as well have left him in the trap. Of course, he's half starved, and still he'd rather run away and live on what he can steal than come back and be fed."

"It is his nature to," absently replied Kathleen, as she looked at the clump of hemlocks they were approaching. "Oh, Jack, won't you please get me some of those upper branches that aren't broken? I want a lot to trim the house for Christmas."

"Oh, bother!" he exclaimed. "Do I have to get off my snowshoes and climb up in that jungle this cold day?"

"You don't *have* to; but if you do, we'll get out the chafing dish and cook all the evening if you like."

"This is shocking!" groaned the boy. "Flat bribery!" Then he briskly demanded, "Creamed oysters?"

"A gallon."

"Nut fudge?"

"A peck!" was the impressive answer.

"All right—that's my price. Another good man gone wrong!" and he tore off his snowshoes and scrambled up toward the best branches, where he broke off the feathery ends and showered them down on Kathleen as she stood with outstretched hands. She made an exceedingly pretty picture, so much so, indeed, that the matter-of-fact fraternal mind was impressed.

"You look stunning, Sis. Better get a green party dress. Here, hold still a minute," as he broke a larger branch. "I'll throw this so the end won't hit you, and it will make a regular opera cloak," and he tossed it with accurate aim. But in doing so he overbalanced himself, and Kathleen, with a scream, saw him sway, catch vainly at the limbs, and fall on the snow, or rather into it. She held her breath as she rushed to him, but after all, she thought, it was hardly possible for anyone to be seriously hurt by falling through the thick foliage of a hemlock into four feet of snow. Though she was startled, she really expected to hear his infectious laugh and a merry comment on his grace and agility; but he lay ominously still, and she saw to her horror that the unexpected had happened.

His head must have struck a limb as he fell, for there was a cut from which the blood was slowly oozing, and he was quite unconscious. She slipped her hand inside his coat and found that his heart was beating, and then, though faint with terror, she bound up his head as well as she could with their two handkerchiefs, drew him over on the hemlock boughs to keep him from the chill of the snow, and pulled off her coat to lay over him, wondering desperately what she could do. She must leave him and go for help; and yet, though home was hardly half a mile away, her heart stood still as she thought of the coyote track. If Jack's old pet was near, others might be; and indeed she believed the brute they had fed would be as likely as another to attack his master. How could she leave him? And still, what would become of him if she did not? The only alternative that she could think of was to make a fire of the hemlock boughs on the side of the wood that could be seen from home, in the hope that someone would come to investigate, though she realized miserably that, even if it was seen, the chances were that it would simply be taken as evidence that she and Jack were enjoying a lark of some kind.

Their establishment consisted only of an unimaginative hired man, a maidservant, Christine, and their old nurse, Norah, who had long been used to having the children, as she still called them, absent for hours in the wildest weather, while their father, though he was proud of and indulgent to them, seldom worried about anything but his own health. Indeed, he had an abiding faith in their ability to take care of themselves, which had been fully justified till now.

Kathleen was at her wit's end; but as she turned, the tears running down her cheeks, to try the poor resource of a fire, she was greeted by a gruff voice inquiring stolidly, "Boy hurt?" and, turning, saw an old French trapper, who had been interesting to her and Jack on account of possessing the only dog team in that part of the country. He had been much ridiculed by his more advanced neighbors, who had risen to the dignity of the ownership of a forlorn mule or horse, but he stubbornly clung to his primitive means of transportation, on the grounds that, as he did no farming, he did not need a team to plow with, and for all other purposes preferred his dogs. His choice seemed a peculiarly happy one in this winter of deep snow, when the heavier draft animals were useless, and their owners, if they wished to go abroad from their isolated claims, had to do so on snowshoes or skis, seeing, perhaps, old Peter luxuriously riding over the snow behind his light-footed team.

His name may have been Pierre to begin with. It had been hardened into its present uncompromising form by Anglo-Saxon neighbors; and, whether from the same cause or not, his disposition was as far as possible from that of the lightsome *voyageur* of song and tale, having, in fact, reverted closely to the original Indian type. However, no cultured heir of all the ages could have been more welcome to Kathleen.

"Oh, Peter!" she cried, "I was never so glad to see anyone in my life! Can you take Jack home on your sled?"

Peter considered a moment, then briefly directed, "You get on sled; hold boy," and assisted in the transfer, his benevolence possibly made active by the memory, and hope, of sundry satisfying meals enjoyed in the Markham kitchen. He then shod himself with Jack's discarded snowshoes, and, taking his place at the head of the leader of his team, started.

Kathleen's relief had left her faint, and the sled having no superfluous room, she confidently expected to fall off; but her strength quickly came back, and so skillfully and rapidly did Peter pilot his equipage, that soon they were safely at their own door.

Norah and Christine came out in surprise that changed to fright when they saw Jack's helpless form and bandaged head, but Kathleen was herself again.

"Speak quietly," she said, "we won't disturb Father if we can help it. Peter, will you please help them carry Jack up to his room? I'll watch the dogs"; and she stood by them till he came back.

"Now Christine will give you a lunch and find some scraps for the dogs," she began, but he interrupted her, declining refreshment for the first time in her acquaintance with him.

"No, Peter go home. Goin' be big snow; come eat some day pretty soon," and, pocketing the silver that Kathleen gratefully offered him, quickly departed.

Looking at the sky as she turned to go in, she saw the heavy clouds that had come up so quickly, and the fine flakes that had already begun to sift down, and realized that Peter's haste was wise.

I must start Ole to the fort for the doctor, she thought as she ran upstairs to help Norah. They soon had Jack safely in bed, but with no sign of returning consciousness.

"I can't make it out," said Norah. "That isn't such an awful bad cut, and he ain't hurt anywhere else, but he just don't come to. I guess Peter'd better go and fetch the doctor."

"Peter wouldn't stay," said Kathleen. "Ole must go over."

"Gracious me!" sharply exclaimed the old nurse, "Ole's gone to see his mother, and your father told him he needn't come back till morning!" The women stared at each other.

But Kathleen spoke with decision. "Then *I* must go. If I were here, I couldn't do anything for Jack that you can't do, and Father needn't know anything about it. He'll have supper in his room, as usual, and you mustn't even tell him that Jack is hurt, if you can help it. I hope I'll be back by the time he comes into the library."

But Norah shook her head. "You mustn't try to go over with those crazy broncos. There's a blizzard coming up if ever I saw the beginning of one, and it's not fit for you to be out."

"No," said Kathleen, quietly, "I shan't try to drive the horses. I'm going to walk. It isn't a mile and a half, and the stage road is well broken now. I'll sling the snowshoes over my shoulder, so that I can put them on if it snows and drifts enough to spoil the road; and I'll take the closed lantern and the compass and a revolver." And then, as the nurse looked unconvinced, she blazed out, "Do you think I'd stay at home and let Jack die without help? And can anyone else go, you or Father? And Christine would sit down in the first drift and announce, 'I die, I die!' And she probably would die! No, I *must* go!"

Norah had not been with Kathleen sixteen years for nothing. She knew that when that young person, ordinarily biddable and sweet tempered enough, "took the bit in her teeth," she was "ill to guide," and she now concluded to hold her tongue. Then, too, she was extremely anxious about Jack.

"He does need the doctor bad," she reflected, "and Kathleen will get over there if any woman that ain't an Indian can."

So she helped the girl make her few preparations and held the door open as she stepped eagerly out into the storm.

It was dark already. The snow was falling thickly, and the wind was rising.

"It isn't a blizzard yet," said Kathleen, brightly, "and see, Norah, the wind is straight behind me. That will make it easy to walk, and the road won't drift as it would with the wind blowing from either side. Take good care of Jack, and I'll have the doctor here in two hours," and she quickly walked away. The house with its outbuildings and then the hemlocks would shield her from the wind at first, but there would be three-quarters of a mile to go over the open prairie. She knew it would be a hard pull, but instead of fear, she felt a wild exultation at being out in the night, doing something to help her merry, loyal playmate. Her delight in their out-of-doors amusements since they had come to the West had more than once led her father laughingly to say that he believed she must have some forgotten Indian or Gypsy ancestor from whom she had inherited the wild strain in her blood, and she began to think tonight that it really must be so, for she was conscious that, even beyond her overmastering desire to bring aid to Jack, she felt a mad response in every vein to the swirl of the wind above the trees and a proud assurance that she could get to the fort safely, no matter how hard it snowed.

Even if it became a blizzard, she *knew* she could crouch and crawl, if necessary, to reach her goal as tirelessly as any Indian, escaped from his captors, would push on to his home.

Suddenly she was sure that she heard a soft sound of a different quality from her own footfall or the wind sweeping through the hemlocks. She turned, and, coming out of the shelter of the trees, she saw an ominously wolfish form against the snow. Her hand went quickly to her revolver, but in another moment she laughed outright.

"Jack's coyote again," she said. "Come here, Modoc; you may go with me if you want to."

It seemed at first as if the prowling beast were inclined to accept her invitation, for he silently glided along in front of her while the woods sheltered them; but as they passed these and the full fury of the snow-laden wind struck them, he stopped, shook himself, and prudently retired to cover again.

"Good night!" called the girl. "Come home tomorrow and I'll give you some bones!" Then she steadied herself for the real work that lay before her.

As she had foreseen, the wind, being directly in line with the road, cleared the track of the new snow rather than drifting any into it, and, blowing from behind her, assisted her progress, though it, more than once, made her stagger. But she went on with an odd sense of freedom. A line of Kipling's that Jack liked to repeat came into her head, and her feet moved lightly to its rhythm:

"And the Northern Lights come down o' nights to dance with the
   houseless snow."

Fantastic ideas drifted through her mind. *The Northern Lights being unavoidably detained,* she idly thought, *I am the fortunate substitute at this ball; but I should call the wind, instead of snow, my partner; no—I am dancing with the snow, and the wind is the music. It certainly quite carries us away*—as a stronger blast almost lifted her from her feet, for its force was constantly increasing.

The road was still good, however, and her exhilaration grew as she hurried on till, in what seemed to her a very short time, she reached the spot where the road turned at right angles to avoid a swamp. Twenty rods ahead were thick hemlocks again, part of the belt that began near her own home and curved in a half circle between them and the fort. At the turn she realized for the first time on what a night she was abroad. The driving snow struck the side of her face and stung and blinded her, and there was no sign of a path to be seen among the drifts. She turned her back to the storm again as she put on her snowshoes, and drew her cap further over her eyes. Then she slowly fought her way in the direction of the dark wall that was often entirely hidden, but which meant shelter for the quarter mile of its width. She would have said that it was hours before she reached it, for the wind seemed to be continually pressing her to one side with invisible but irresistible hands; but at last she was safe in its protection. She leaned against a tree trunk for a minute or two to recover her breath, and then went on confidently for some time till the outline of the track she was taking and the unfamiliar position of the trees made her stop suddenly and look around with the dawning conviction that in her struggle with the wind she had failed to enter the woods at the right point and had been following one of the natural aisles made by the trees, by which every wood wanderer, sooner or later, is deceived.

Her first feeling was of wrath, pure and simple. *To think that I should play such a tenderfoot trick!* she thought. *Now what shall I do? Much good my compass is! It will get me straight east out of the woods, but when I get out, how am I going to tell whether the fort is north or south of me? Anyway, I'll go on through. It wouldn't be any easier to find the right track if I went back, and perhaps I'm not so far out of the way but that I can see the lights when I get to the other side.*

So she opened the lantern, looked at her compass, and then went on till the belt of trees was crossed. Then she strained her eyes eagerly to see the fort, but there was no light or sign of life. The snow drifted down heavily, relentlessly, in the lee of the woods, but beyond them, where the wind struck it, it whirled, plunged, and fled before the furious blast. The contour of the rolling prairie was strange to Kathleen, and resembled in no way the familiar slopes and hollows of the country near the fort, while there was absolutely nothing to show her in which direction she ought to go.

But she was not long in deciding. *I must follow the edge of the woods south for a quarter of a mile, and then, if I see nothing that looks natural, I must come back and go as much farther north. I surely can find the fort that way, if I have to go back and forth all night. But what will Jack do in the meantime? And how frightened they will be about me!* The thought spurred her to instant motion, but as she started south, she heard a low whine, and near her, between the closely growing trees, she again saw a familiar outline, fawning in the most apologetic manner. Kathleen's gaze was one of blank amazement.

"What in the world—why, Modoc, is that you?"

Another whine seemed to indicate an affirmative answer.

"Why, then it wasn't you I saw before. You'd never have crossed the prairie in the storm—though of course, you could have come around through the trees. I suppose you could easily make more than three times the ground that I do."

Still she was incredulous and puzzled. The coyote had done some queer things in the way of tracking and following them in the brief period when they had considered him domesticated, but that had been more than a month ago, and they supposed that he had forgotten by this time whatever feeling of intimacy and confidence he might have learned, though all the old settlers agreed that never before had anyone made so much of a success in taming one of his supposedly untamable tribe.

The coyote whined again, and, looking back at the girl, started north, then stopped, and, Kathleen was sure, waited for her to follow. She shrugged her shoulders. Did he mean to try to induce her to accompany him to the home of one of his numerous relatives? She was by no means sure of the friendliness of his intentions, but concluded that she might as well follow him, for the quarter of a mile she had allowed herself, in that direction as well as the other. She could keep in sight of the open country, and at worst she had her revolver, while at best—she suddenly remembered that some of the cooks at the fort had reported having seen an astonishingly tame coyote occasionally skirmishing around their scrap pails, and she began to hope that that might be his destination. So she followed him for much more than a quarter of a mile, till he turned to the open, and, lifting his head, gave voice to a low howl. Looking in the direction in which he was headed, she began to see something familiar in the dim outlines she was facing. As she peered intently through the almost opaque whiteness, her eyes caught a faint glimmer of light, and she knew that she was only a short distance from the fort.

It was with a very grateful heart that she turned to Modoc, but that enterprising animal had disappeared without waiting for any acknowledgment of his eminent services.

Afterward, when Kathleen told her tale of the strange guide who had led her to safety, she was greeted with derision and incredulity among those who claimed to have an intimate acquaintance with the coyote family. One old resident of the country voiced the unanimous opinion of his clan when he said, "Now, Miss Markham, if that critter kept along with you for a ways, it was just because he was looking for you to freeze. There ain't no good in a coyote!" But all their lives Jack and Kathleen believed that it was simple loyalty and gratitude to those who had once saved him from the jaws of a wolf trap that brought him to his friend's aid.

As Kathleen came out of the lee of the hemlocks, she found that the storm had undoubtedly reached the blizzard mark. It was harder work now to go forward than when the road had first turned, but the occasional gleam of light that reached her served both to encourage and guide her, and though she was panting for breath when she at last reached the door of the old army surgeon, she felt little exhaustion. When that gentleman himself opened the door, and she saw his astounded face as he recognized her, she almost laughed.

"Why, Kathleen, child," he declared, seizing her hand and drawing her in at the door, snowshoes and all, "where did you drop from this terrible night? Where's Jack?"

"Jack's had a bad fall and is unconscious," she answered, "and I'm here to ask you please to come to him at once."

"Of course," said he, "but not on snowshoes, thank you—and do you mean to say that you came alone?"

"Not entirely. Jack's coyote was with me at times, and a splendid escort he was."

"Well!" gasped the amazed doctor, "I don't see how you ever got over here alive. What on earth was your father thinking of to let you start out?"

"He didn't know I was coming—but, oh, Doctor, *do* come back with me as soon as you can!"

"Surely I will, but I need more of an escort than a coyote. We'll have a sleigh and two horses and two soldiers to manage them. I'll have them ready in five minutes," he replied, as he went to the telephone to give directions, and then asked minute questions as to Jack's injury, nodding at Kathleen's answers with a reassuring smile. "We'll soon bring him round all right. Don't worry."

The journey back in the teeth of the wind took much longer than the walk to the fort. The stalwart soldiers who led the team had to throw blankets over the horses' heads before they would face the storm, and there were deep drifts to be trampled down ahead of them. Twice they lost the road and wandered out on the prairie where the wind had scooped deceptive hollows that looked like traveled paths, but which ended in impassable mountains of snow.

But at last they reached the friendly shelter of the hemlocks, and in a few minutes were at the house. Jack, very much alive and animated, was the first to greet them.

"Kathleen Markham," he said severely, "I'd like to pummel you! And I hope Dad will! It's about time for him to come down to the library, and you can do the explaining. Did you suppose a little crack on the head was going to hurt *me*? There never was a girl like you, Sis!" he added in a different tone as he hurriedly and rather shamefacedly bent to kiss her, having ascertained by a backward glance that the doctor had turned to speak to his father, who had just come from his room.

"Now, Kathleen, I'll fire up the chafing dish, and let's have those creamed oysters!"

* * * * *

"Through the Storm," by Mary Woodbury Caswell. Published March 1916 in St. Nicholas. Mary Woodbury Caswell wrote for popular magazines during the first third of the twentieth century.

Faithful Unto Death

John Morris

Out of four baby crows, he was the only one to stay by them—because of this, they named him Faithful. Little did they then realize the real significance of that name!

* * * * *

An explosion of gunpowder was heard, and four orphans were left at the mercy of the world, to live or die, as chance might decree. The next day after the cruel instrument of destruction had done its work, I heard a noise in the top of a tall tree. I looked up, and there I saw a nest. To my surprise, I discovered that it had four baby crows in it.

Since the father and mother had been killed by our neighbor's shotgun, I decided to adopt these small orphans as my pets. So I climbed the tree and secured for myself the nest with the four young birds. As this particular tree was thickly covered with thorns, I received several cuts and scratches while making my way to the nest and then back to the ground.

The birds looked like four little balls of fur with porcupine quills scattered here and there. Their sparkling eyes resembled tiny glass beads. These little fellows were about the size of robins, and they seemed very lively in spite of the fact that they had been without food for twenty-four hours.

As I did not know what to feed them, I asked the advice of one of my Indian friends, Ali Baksh. He told me to give them some warm bread and milk, and I did so. They were very hungry and ate ravenously, but I was afraid to feed them too much after their long fast, lest it might kill them. They were fed twice a day, at five in the morning and at the same hour at night, and it was not long before these young crows began to expect their meals at regular times. If five o'clock came and they were not fed, they would all make a great noise and chirp away in a most plaintive tone, as if asking when they would get their food.

One day as I was feeding my pets, Abdulla, another of my Indian friends, became very much interested in the birds and volunteered to help me care for them. Afterward he tended to them the greater part of the time.

These crows grew very rapidly and soon were large enough to climb out of their nest. They made a general nuisance of themselves by getting in the way, and whenever anyone took a step, he was liable to land on a crow.

There was a small deserted house just a few hundred feet away from my home, and I finally decided that it would be best to keep them there where

they would not be in the way or in danger of being hurt by members of the family. One day when I went to visit them, I found the door partly open. A large hound had entered and was chasing my crows all around the room. After he had caught one of them, he stood holding it between his paws, pulling out feathers and biting the baby bird until it was very badly injured. I grabbed a large stick and proceeded to deal with that dog in a manner that I thought was just. Then I took the wounded crow and tried to soothe its cuts. But it did no good; the poor little bird was dead the next morning.

Abdulla and I decided that two crows were enough to care for, and when we had a chance to sell one of the three remaining for three rupees, or about one dollar, we did so.

Our two crows were now large enough to eat whatever they wanted. We fed them worms, grain, and many other things. Also we began to train them to pick up money, pins, needles, and other small articles. They did not like to do this, but we would not feed them until they did, and they soon learned that to obey was the quickest way to get their dinner.

They were very tame by this time, and we allowed them to fly around wherever they pleased. Whenever they would find any small, glittering object, they would pick it up and bring it to me, expecting to be fed. One of the crows took advantage of his liberty and disappeared with his wild friends. We never saw him again, even though we searched everywhere possible. The other one remained a faithful friend till the last, and because of this we called him Faithful.

Although he was very mischievous at times, he was very amusing. Once while I was feeding him he took hold of my nose and shook it as only a crow could. Then he quickly flew away and would not let me feed him anymore that evening. He would sit a few feet away and seem to be laughing at me. Another favorite trick of his was to creep up behind a sleeping dog and grab him by the tail, and then, before the dog could catch him, fly away and caw in great glee. He would never bother a dog while it was awake. Evidently he remembered the time the hound chased him.

Whenever he was in danger he would perch on my shoulder or that of Abdulla. Although he was very talkative, we were unable to understand what he said. The time finally came when I had to leave that part of India, and I asked Abdulla if he would keep him and take good care of him. He said, "*Bashack,*" which means "sure," so I said farewell to my adopted friend.

Three months later, when I was visiting that section for a short while, I stopped in to see my old pet. He immediately hopped to my shoulder and started to tell me in crow language all that had happened since I had gone away. He was always afraid of strangers, but he remembered me at once and seemed very glad to see me. When I prepared to leave, Faithful tried to follow me to the train. He perched on my shoulder, hoping to go with me. I was sorry to part with him, but as he was of great use to Abdulla in keeping the parrots out of the orange groves, I left him there. I shall never forget the look of sadness that he gave me as the train pulled away. He seemed to realize that I was leaving, never to see him again.

It is common practice in India for people to sleep in the open air during the summer, on account of the intense heat. One hot evening when Abdulla was sleeping in the yard, a large cobra crawled up and slept beside his bed during the night. As morning drew near, the cobra roused and raised his head ready to strike any living thing that should move before him. Faithful also awakened and saw the deadly cobra. He flew to the bed of one of Abdulla's companions, who was about ten feet away, and tried to awaken him. The man was so drowsy that he sensed no danger and only threw a pebble at Faithful to drive him away. Just then Abdulla turned in his sleep, and the crow, realizing that the snake was going to strike, took his last chance to save his beloved master. He flew at the serpent and pecked him fiercely on the back. At this the cobra turned away from Abdulla and attacked Faithful. The other man then noticed the poisonous snake and immediately killed it. Faithful died from the snakebite in about half an hour, but Abdulla was saved.

Surely this pet crow was rightly named. He was a faithful friend to the last. He paid the price of friendship in giving his life to protect his master.

* * * * *

"Faithful Unto Death," by John Morris. Published August 6, 1940, in The Youth's Instructor. *Text reprinted by permission of Joe Wheeler (P.O. Box 1246, Conifer, CO 80433) and Review and Herald® Publishing Association, Hagerstown, MD 21740. John Morris wrote for inspirational magazines during the first half of the twentieth century.*

TONY

Eleanor Hammond

His classmates jeered at his nondescript pony. They did, that is, until one memorable winter when a mountain lion went on a rampage.

* * * * *

He was a very ordinary-looking beast. His ancestry, part wild cayuse, part nobody knows what. He was ewe-necked and lean and elderly. His color was a faded bay without variation or distinction. Among the smartly colored pintos and handsome buckskin ponies that were tied in the school shed every day, Tony made a poor appearance. There were twelve boys attending the Brush Hill School. They all, except two from the nearest ranch house, rode ponies and came several miles to acquire an education. They all, except Tim Day, rode better ponies than Tony.

"But he's right smart!" Tim argued loyally. "He knows more than most hosses!"

"You'll have to show us!" was the scoffing decision of Tim's schoolmates.

"He found his way home through a snowstorm when I hadn't any idea which way to go. Saved my life last winter," Tim pointed out.

"Aw, any hoss could do that. They always know the way home," Tom

Barnes insisted. "Tony'll have to do something better than that before you can make me believe he's anything special!"

Doubtless Tony knew very little about the difference of opinion which raged in Brush Hill School because of him. Doubtless he was not setting out to justify Tim's loyal faith in him when he distinguished himself so notably that winter. But the story of Tony and the gray killer is one that Tim and even his elders are proud to tell.

The Day ranch was farther from the school than any other. It was close to ten miles up the side of Lone Mountain. School was in session six months in the summer. During the winter deep snow kept the Day family isolated on their own ranch as completely as if they had been cast away on a desert island. Most of the ranchers in that frontier region were shut in in the same way during the worst weather. In the coulees, snow piled fifty and seventy-five feet deep. The stock shivered and froze in spite of Tim's and his father's efforts to keep them fed. The huge haystacks, cut and piled during the summer, when grass kept the cows and horses fed, dwindled to nothing before the onslaughts of the hungry animals. Oil cake eked out their rations toward spring. Every rancher counted upon losing some stock from cold during the long siege of winter weather. Little heaps under the new snow showed where the dead cows lay, waiting the burial the buzzards would give them in the spring. Winter was a hard time for men and beasts on Lone Mountain.

Tony suffered less from the winter than most of the stock. Tim kept his pony in the sheds during the worst days, and he saw to it that Tony had nourishing oil cake and oats daily.

"It seems to me we're losing a powerful lot of stock this winter," Mr. Day said. "I never knew the cold to take so many."

A closer examination showed that it was not the cold that was causing all the pathetic little graves under the new snow.

"There's blood by that yearling that died last night," Tim's father said one morning. "I wish more snow hadn't fallen—so I could see the tracks of the beast that did the killing!"

A grizzly bear, a wolf, a cougar—it might have been any of them.

"Whatever the killer is, he's a crafty one! He does his wicked work and slides way again like a shadow," the rancher said. "And the worst of it is, he's killing for fun, not just for food. He doesn't eat a quarter of what he kills!"

Stock killers were all too common in that region. A wily beast of prey might cost a rancher hundreds of dollars in good stock in a few nights, and the Days were far from rich.

"We've got to find out what's doing the damage and get him," Mr. Day said.

But this was far easier to say than to do. A line of traps up the mountainside brought no results. Poisoned meat did not seem to tempt the cattle killer. The Days drove all their little band of stock into the sheds and corrals. Still colts and calves, even full-grown horses, were found slaughtered inside the very corral fences.

"I'm going to sit up all night with my rifle and wait for that varmint by the corral fence!" Mr. Day declared.

But his all-night vigil in the cold was useless. The wary killer caught the human smell on the keen air and tiptoed away silently. The tracks on the snow below the corrals showed the killer was a mountain lion.

"I'm going to get him before he gets Tony!" Tim said determinedly. It was well known that cougars like horse meat, and Tony was a small beast—an easy prey for a mountain lion bent on destruction.

"You can try, son," Mr. Day said, "but it'll be a miracle if any of us get him."

A night spent in the shed where Tony and the other horses were housed, left Tim with some frosted fingertips, but no sight of the killer. Tim's mother insisted that the boy should not repeat the attempt to shoot the cougar that way.

It was the very next night that a shrill human-sounding scream woke Tim from his deepest sleep. The sound had certainly come from the horse shed. Tim leaped from the bed and pulled on enough clothes to cross the snowy space between the ranch house and the barn.

The scream echoed through the night again. Tim snatched down the gun from its rack over the door and dashed out into the night. The scream was certainly Tony's!

By the thin light of a sinking moon, Tim made his way into the shed. The door had been smashed open and the lock broken.

As the boy came into the low building, a huge catlike thing leaped through the farthest window, smashing the glass as it went. Tim fired with a shaking hand. The bullet went wild and hit the rafters.

Tim hurried to the place where Tony had been tied. He nearly cried with relief when he found the bay pony safe. In the next stall a fine colt lay with its skull crushed by a blow from the mountain lion's paw.

"You were calling me to come! You were calling me!" Tim told Tony, with his arms around the skinny neck. "Well, we'll get the old killer yet! We'll get him and put a stop to his work!"

It was with this determination that Tim set out up the mountainside a few weeks later. A quick thaw had melted the snow from the ridges and made riding possible. There was a flavor of spring in the air that made both the boy and the pony glad to be outdoors. Fresh tracks from the corrals pointed unmistakably to the fact that the dreaded killer had gone in this direction.

But the day wore away, and no more definite signs of the cougar came in sight. The sun began to sink toward the horizon and the night to approach. Still Tim had seen nothing to make him feel he was on the right track.

"I suppose we'd better turn back, old boy," Tim said to his pony. "I reckon Dad was right saying it would be a wild-goose chase to try to find that cougar in daylight."

Tony whinnied knowingly as they turned down the mountain. He hastened his pace. He was glad to be headed back for home and a good meal.

But Tim had ridden a long way in his enthusiasm for finding the killer. Long before he was anywhere near home, the sun was below the horizon. A few frosty stars came out, and they were blotted out by shifting clouds. The ground was freezing again, and Tony's hoofs slid dangerously on the steep places.

Finally the old pony slipped and fell to his knees. He struggled up with difficulty. His knees were badly skinned. He looked around and gave a low, pleading whinny as if to say, *Why do you make me go on when the ground is like this?*

It was nearly dark now, and Tim blamed himself severely for having gone so far. "There's no help for it, though, old pal," he told Tony. "We'll have to take it slow and try to get there. Mother will worry if we're out all night."

Suddenly Tony became nervous and jumpy. He rolled his eyes and snorted strangely. He tried to hurry, but the slippery slopes made that almost impossible, despite his efforts.

"What's the matter, Tony? What do you smell?" Tim asked. He always talked to his pony quite as if Tony could understand, and Tony did understand a surprising amount.

Then a slinking shadow slipping behind some brush told Tim what had caused the horse's nervousness. Tony had good reason for alarm. The shadow was that of a huge beast, probably the killer cougar himself.

Tim's heart began to pound. He tried to get enough sight of the animal to fire his rifle. He must make sure his shot was fatal, for a wounded cougar might attack.

Tim slid from his pony's back. Tony nickered nervously.

The killer was nowhere in sight now.

"I'll build a fire and wait for him. We can't go on and have him jump on us from some overhanging rock," Tim decided. Besides, he knew Tony might be too filled with panic to go forward safely and cautiously with that shadow trailing them.

There was plenty of dead wood from the scrub pines near the spot to furnish fuel. Tim threw the reins over Tony's head and began collecting wood. He always carried matches for kindling campfires, and he whittled a pitchy stick into fine shavings. Soon he had a comfortable blaze burning. Tony edged close. He, too, was glad of the warmth. Maybe he, too, realized that the wild enemy would not come near fire.

For an hour and then another hour, Tim kept the blaze burning. He moved cautiously about the vicinity, hoping for a sight of the cougar and a chance to shoot. But the killer seemed to have left the neighborhood.

Tim thought regretfully, of the worry his parents would feel at his absence, but there was no help for it. His only safety under the circumstances lay in staying by the protecting fire till daylight.

The boy piled more wood on and sat down to wait for the darkness to pass. He collected a large pile of fuel. There would be enough to keep up the fire, if only he could keep awake. After eating the last of the lunch he had carried in his pockets, Tim began to feel warm and sleepy. He was not used to staying awake all night. Tim's head nodded—and nodded again.

He sat up with a start. Something had waked him from sleep.

Then he realized what it was. It was Tony's soft cold nose touching his face. Tony's teeth were holding his collar. Tony was gently shaking his master awake.

The fire was nearly out. Tim hastily piled more branches on it and blew on the coals to revive the flame.

He patted Tony's nose. "Good old pal! You knew we mustn't sleep here in the dark with no fire to keep the cougar away, didn't you? You're smart, you are!"

Again Tim settled himself comfortably in the circle of light and warmth. It seemed as if the night would never come to an end. Tom nodded once more. Again the fire sunk low. Again the wise old pony shook him awake to replenish the blaze.

The first gray of dawn was streaking the sky when Tim was awakened sharply in a different manner. Tony was shaking him violently this time. There was no gentleness in his manner. Tim started up, half annoyed with the pony's insistence. Tony was quivering all over, but he was perfectly silent.

Tim rubbed his eyes and looked around. He smothered a cry of surprise and alarm. He reached for his rifle.

There in the brush at the other side of the fire was a pair of shining cat eyes. They seemed to burn red with the light reflected in their pupils from the fire.

Crouching—all ready to spring at us! Tim thought.

In the second between the time when Tony woke him and the time his rifle shot echoed through the brush, the boy's mind was working very fast. Here was his chance at last—the chance they had been waiting for all winter— the chance to end the killing of the harmless cattle and horses by this cruel beast of prey. Yet—if he missed?

It would be easy enough to scare the cougar away, probably. Cougars seldom attacked human beings, especially when they were faced boldly and shouted at. Only a man who was down already need fear the deliberate attack from such an animal as this. But a wounded cougar—that would be a very different matter. The old rifle was a single shot gun. Would he have time to reload it if he missed a fatal shot the first time? It was not probable he would have time.

"I've got to get him! Got to!" Tim set his jaw. "I can't let him go on killing our stock!"

But the boy's hand shook as he took aim and fired.

There was a furious snarling cry from the creature in the brush. Tim knew he had hit the cougar, and the shot had not been fatal!

The next moment Tim himself gave a cry of alarm. The maddened beast was coming toward him. It was going to attack!

The cougar was springing forward unsteadily in a queer lopsided way. It was badly wounded, but far from completely disabled. Its long cat teeth gleamed viciously as it came.

Tim's hand fumbled for another cartridge. He hadn't time to get it into the gun. It was too late.

With a quick jump, he avoided the oncoming claws. He dashed down the mountainside. The cougar had missed in its spring. It was recovering now to renew its attack.

Then Tim's foot slipped on the icy ground. He fell facedown. He clutched at the earth with frantic fingers. He went on, falling over a low ledge. Then he was rolling helplessly down—down. His head struck a scrub pine root, and everything went black.

It was several minutes before the boy regained his senses enough to realize where he was. He was bruised, but uninjured otherwise, lying several hundred feet down the mountain from the embers of his fire.

Tim scrambled up and looked for his gun. It was nowhere near. He moved back toward the fire cautiously. Suddenly he was filled with concern for his pony. Tony was not in sight.

"Could that cougar have got him?" Tim hurried on. His heart sank. He picked up his rifle from near the fire and started the search.

Then suddenly, a soft, cold nose thrust against his neck from behind made the boy turn with a glad cry. He flung his arms round Tony's skinny neck. "You're safe! You're all right, old boy?" Tim cried.

But there was a cruel gash from long claws on Tony's flank and another on his foreleg. They would heal, but Tony would always wear the scars.

"Where's that cougar? I'll get him now!" Tim grasped his gun.

Then, a hundred feet from the place where he stood, he saw all that was left of the cruel killer. The killer would kill no more. He was a trampled mass of tawny hide, and there was blood on Tony's hoofs. Tony had finished the job his master's bullet had begun. He had trampled the killer to death.

* * * * *

"Tony," by Eleanor Hammond. Published October 21, 1931, in The Youth's Instructor. *Text reprinted by permission of Joe Wheeler (P.O. Box 1246, Conifer, CO 80433) and Review and Herald® Publishing Association, Hagerstown, MD 21740. Eleanor Hammond wrote for inspirational and popular magazines during the first half of the twentieth century.*

THE CAT THAT FED A PRISONER

A. H. Cannon

Despondently, the young prisoner took stock of his options. There were virtually none; he was dying of starvation, and there was nothing he could do about it.

Or so he thought.

* * * * *

Alice, Ruth, and Ted had listened attentively while Mother told them the story of Elijah and God's protecting care for him and how He had fed Elijah by means of the ravens.

Ruth sat looking at her mother with a somewhat puzzled expression.

"Well, what are you thinking about, Ruth?" inquired Mother.

Ruth hesitated a moment, but Mother's reassuring smile brought confidence to her little daughter. "We read that God could care for and feed Elijah in such a remarkable way in Bible times, yet we do not hear of His feeding people in the same remarkable way in our time."

"Yes, Ruth, we are so apt to think that, but God still provides for His children the same as He did for Elijah. I will tell you a story that occurred long ago in England.

"This experience took place at the time when the Britons were engaged in that famous civil war called the War of the Roses. The two parties concerned each took a rose for its emblem—one a red rose, the other a white rose.

"Now, in that beautiful part of England known to so many people as the Garden of England lived a wealthy lord who belonged to the House of Lancaster. He was of the party that wore a red rose. He had to leave his lovely home in Kent and allow himself to be taken prisoner and placed in a cold and narrow tower.

"That prison with its cold, dark, and damp little room was not the only discomfort the poor man had to endure. Sir Henry Wyatt, for that was his

name, had no bed to lie on; but the worst thing of all was the lack of food.

"One day when Sir Henry was sitting in his cramped quarters, chilled to the bone—for his clothes weren't thick enough to protect him in his chilly prison—his thoughts went to God and Elijah, and he prayed that the Lord would sustain him.

"Sir Henry had just finished his prayer when he received an unannounced visitor, but nevertheless welcome. It was a cat which had entered by the window. Sir Henry cuddled it, and its soft fur warmed his chilled body. When the cat thought she'd stayed long enough, she left by the same way that she came.

"But the cat did not forget Sir Henry, for it returned the next day, but this time it brought a pigeon in its mouth. This gladdened Sir Henry, but the next problem was how to prepare it so that he could eat it. So when the jailer visited him next time, Sir Henry complained about his food. 'I dare not better it,' said the man.

" 'But if I can provide anything, will you dress and cook it for me?' asked Sir Henry.

"The jailer thought that it was impossible for his prisoner to get anything, so he consented to do it for him. Sir Henry then handed over the pigeon to him. The man looked bewildered, but he kept his promise, although he was afraid of being caught by his superiors. This fear, however, left him after he had done it a number of times.

"And so Sir Henry Wyatt was saved from starvation, for this cat continued bringing a portion of food until the day came when he was released from prison. Afterward, Wyatt became a personal friend of King Henry VII. But in all the prosperity that attended him at his castle in Allington in Kent, Sir Henry Wyatt always remembered with gratitude to God the way he was fed in the days of his deep need and privation.

"So, children," said Mother, "You can see that God is still willing to use His mighty power on our behalf if we will only have faith enough to ask and believe that He will do it."

* * * * *

"The Cat That Fed a Prisoner," by A. H. Cannon. If anyone knows the original source of this old story or the whereabouts of the author's next of kin, please send the information to Joe Wheeler (P.O. Box 1246, Conifer, CO 80433).

LITTLE WARHORSE

Ernest Thompson Seton

He was just a rabbit, one of the most defenseless animals on the planet—yet Jack somehow survived—and survived—and survived.
But finally, his luck ran out.
Or so his enemies thought.

* * * * *

So impressed was Ernest Thompson Seton with the story of this most remarkable of rabbits that he included it in his famous book, Animal Heroes.

* * * * *

I

The Little Warhorse knew practically all the Dogs in town. First, there was a very large brown Dog that had pursued him many times, a Dog that he always got rid of by slipping through a hole in a board fence. Second, there was a small active Dog that could follow through that hole, and him he baffled by leaping a twenty-foot irrigation ditch that had steep sides and a swift current. The Dog could not make this leap. It was "sure medicine" for that

foe, and the boys still call the place "Old Jacky's Jump." But there was a Greyhound that could leap better than the Jack, and when he could not follow through a fence, he jumped over it. He tried the Warhorse's mettle more than once, and Jacky only saved himself by his quick dodging, till they got to an Osage orange hedge, and here the Greyhound had to give it up. Besides these, there was in town a rabble of big and little Dogs that were troublesome, but easily left behind in the open.

In the country there was a Dog at each farmhouse, but only one that the Warhorse really feared; that was a long-legged, fierce, black Dog, a brute so swift and pertinacious that he had several times forced the Warhorse almost to the last extremity.

For the town Cats he cared little; only once or twice had he been threatened by them. A huge tomcat flushed with many victories came crawling up to where he fed one moonlight night. Jack Warhorse saw the black creature with the glowing eyes, and a moment before the final rush, he faced it, raised up on his haunches, his hind legs, at full length on his toes, with his broad ears towering up yet six inches higher; then letting out a loud *churrr-churrr,* his best attempt at a roar, he sprang five feet forward and landed on the Cat's head, driving in his sharp hind nails, and the old Tom fled in terror from the weird two-legged giant. This trick he had tried several times with success, but twice it turned out a sad failure: once, when the Cat proved to be a mother whose kittens were near, then Jack Warhorse had to flee for his life; and the other time was when he made the mistake of landing hard on a Skunk.

But the Greyhound was the dangerous enemy, and in him the Warhorse might have found his fate, but for a curious adventure with a happy ending for Jack.

He fed by night; there were fewer enemies about then, and it was easier to hide. But one day at dawn in winter he had lingered long at an alfalfa stack and was crossing the open snow toward his favorite form, when, as ill luck would have it, he met the Greyhound prowling outside the town. With open snow and growing daylight, there was no chance to hide, nothing but a run in the open with soft snow that hindered the Jack more than it did the Hound.

Off they went—superb runners in fine fettle. How they skimmed across the snow, raising it in little *puff puff puffs,* each time their nimble feet went down. This way and that, swerving and dodging, went the chase. Everything favored the Dog—his empty stomach, the cold weather, the soft snow—while the Rabbit was handicapped by his heavy meal of alfalfa. But his feet went *puff puff* so fast that a dozen of the little snow jets were in view at once. The chase continued in the open; no friendly hedge was near, and every attempt to reach a fence was cleverly stopped by the Hound. Jack's ears were losing their bold up-cock, a sure sign of failing heart or wind, when all at once these flags went stiffly up, as under sudden renewal of strength. The Warhorse put forth all his power, not to reach the hedge to the north, but over the open prairie eastward. The Greyhound followed, and within fifty yards the Jack dodged to foil his fierce pursuer; but on the next tack he was on his eastern course again, and so tacking and dodging, he kept the line direct for the next farmhouse, where was a very high board fence with a hen hole, and where also there dwelt his other hated enemy, the big black Dog. An outer hedge delayed the Greyhound for a moment and gave Jack time to dash through the hen hole into the yard, where he hid to one side. The Greyhound rushed around to the low gate, leaped over that among the Hens, and as they fled, cackling and fluttering, some Lambs bleated loudly. Their natural guardian, the big black Dog, ran to the rescue, and Warhorse slipped out again by the hole at which he had entered. Horrible sounds of Dog hate and fury were heard behind him in the hen yard, and soon the shouts of men were added. How it ended he did not know or seek to learn, but it was remarkable that he never afterward was troubled by the swift Greyhound that formerly lived in Newchusen.

II

Hard times and easy times had long followed in turn and been taken as matters of course; but recent years in the state of Kaskado had brought to the Jackrabbits a succession of remarkable ups and downs. In the old days they had their endless fight with Birds and Beasts of Prey, with cold and heat, with pestilence and with flies whose sting bred a loathsome disease, and yet had held their own. But the settling of the country by farmers made many changes.

Dogs and guns arriving in numbers reduced the ranks of Coyotes, Foxes, Wolves, Badgers, and Hawks that preyed on the Jacks, so that in a few years the Rabbits were multiplied in great swarms; but now Pestilence broke out and swept them away. Only the strongest—the double seasoned—remained.

For a while a Jackrabbit was a rarity; but during this time another change came in. The Osage orange hedges planted everywhere afforded a new refuge, and now the safety of a Jackrabbit was less often his speed than his wits, and the wise ones, when pursued by a Dog or Coyote, would rush to the nearest hedge through a small hole and escape while the enemy sought for a larger one by which to follow. The Coyotes rose to this and developed the trick of the relay chase. In this, one Coyote takes one field, another the next, and if the Rabbit attempts the hedge ruse they work from each side and usually win their prey. The Rabbit remedy for this is keen eyes to see the second Coyote, avoidance of that field, then good legs to distance the first enemy.

Thus the Jackrabbits, after being successively numerous, scarce, in myriads, and rare, were now again on the increase, and those which survived, selected by a hundred hard trials, were enabled to flourish where their ancestors could not have outlived a single season.

Their favorite grounds were not the broad open stretches of the big ranches, but the complicated, much-fenced fields of the farms, where these were so small and close as to be like a big straggling village.

One of these vegetable villages had sprung up around the railway station of Newchusen. The country a mile away was well supplied with jackrabbits of the new and selected stock. Among them was a little lady Rabbit called "Bright Eyes," from her leading characteristic as she sat gray in the gray brush. She was a good runner, but was especially successful with the fence play that baffled the Coyotes. She made her nest out in an open pasture, an untouched tract of ancient prairie. Here her brood were born and raised. One like herself was bright eyed, in coat of silver gray, and partly gifted with her ready wits, but in the other, there appeared a rare combination of his mother's gifts with the best that was in the best strain of the new Jackrabbits of the plains.

This was the one whose adventures we have been following, the one that later on the turf won the name of Little Warhorse and that afterward achieved a worldwide fame.

Ancient tricks of his kind he revived and put to new uses, and ancient enemies he learned to fight with newfound tricks.

When a mere baby he discovered a plan that was worthy of the wisest Rabbit in Kaskado. He was pursued by a horrible little Yellow Dog, and he had tried in vain to get rid of him by dodging among the fields and farms. This is a good play against a Coyote, because the farmers and the Dogs will often help the Jack, without knowing it, by attacking the Coyote. But now the plan did not work at all, for the little Dog managed to keep after him through one fence after another, and Jack Warhorse, not yet full grown, much less seasoned, was beginning to feel the strain. His ears were no longer up straight, but angling back and at times drooping to a level, as he darted through a very little hole in an Osage hedge, only to find that his nimble enemy had done the same without loss of time. In the middle of the field was a small herd of cattle and with them was a Calf.

There is in wild animals a curious impulse to trust any stranger when in desperate straits. The foe behind they know means death. There is just a chance, and the only one left, that the stranger may prove friendly; and it was this last desperate chance that drew Jack Warhorse to the Cows.

It is quite sure that the Cows would have stood by in stolid indifference so far as the Rabbit was concerned, but they have a deep-rooted hatred of a Dog, and when they saw the Yellow Cur coming bounding toward them, their tails and noses went up; they sniffed angrily, then closed up ranks, and led by the Cow that owned the Calf, they charged at the Dog, while Jack took refuge under a low thornbush. The Dog swerved aside to attack the Calf, at least the old Cow thought he did, and she followed him so fiercely that he barely escaped from that field with his life.

It was a good old plan—one that doubtless came from the days when Buffalo and Coyote played the parts of Cow and Dog. Jack never forgot it, and more than once it saved his life.

In color as well as in power, he was a rarity.

Animals are colored in one or other of two general plans: one that matches them with their surroundings and helps them to hide—this is called "protective"; the other that makes them very visible for several purposes—this is called "directive." Jackrabbits are peculiar in being painted both ways. As they squat in their form in the gray brush or clods, they are soft gray on their ears, head, back, and sides; they match the ground and cannot be seen until close at hand—they are *protectively* colored. But the moment it is clear to the Jack that the approaching foe will find him, he jumps up and dashes away. He throws off all the disguise now, the gray seems to disappear; he makes a lightning change, and his ears show snowy white with black tips, the legs are white, his tail is a black spot in a blaze of white. He is a black-and-white Rabbit now. His coloring is all *directive.* How is it done? Very simply. The front side of the ear is gray, the back, black and white. The black tail with its white halo, and the legs, are tucked below. He is sitting on them. The gray mantle is pulled down and enlarged as he sits, but when he jumps up it shrinks somewhat, all his black-and-white marks are now shown, and just as his colors formerly whispered, "I am a clod," they now shout aloud, "I am a Jackrabbit."

Why should he do this? Why should a timid creature running for his life thus proclaim to all the world his name instead of trying to hide? There must be some good reason. It must pay, or the Rabbit would never have done it. The answer is, if the creature that scared him up was one of his own kind, i.e., this was a false alarm, then at once, by showing his national colors, the mistake is made right. On the other hand, if it be a Coyote, Fox, or Dog, they see at once, this is a Jackrabbit and know that it would be waste of time for them to pursue him. They say, in effect, "This is a Jackrabbit, and I cannot catch a Jack in open race." They give it up, and that, of course, saves the Jack a great deal of unnecessary running and worry. The black-and-white spots are the national uniform and flag of the Jacks. In poor specimens they are apt to be dull, but in the finest specimens they are not only larger, but brighter than usual, and the Little Warhorse, gray when he sat in his form, blazed like charcoal and snow when he flung his defiance to the Fox and buff Coyote and danced with little effort before them, first a black-and-white Jack, then a little white spot, and last a speck of thistledown, before the distance swallowed him.

Many of the farmers' Dogs had learned the lesson: a grayish Rabbit you may catch, but a very black-and-white one is hopeless. They might, indeed, follow for a time, but that was merely for the fun of a chivy, and his growing power often led Warhorse to seek the chase for the sake of a little excitement, and to take hazards that others less gifted were most careful to avoid.

Jack, like all other wild animals, had a certain range or country which was home to him, and outside of this he rarely strayed. It was about three miles across, extending easterly from the center of the village. Scattered through this he had a number of "forms," or "beds" as they are locally called. These were mere hollows situated under a sheltering bush or bunch of grass, without lining excepting the accidental grass and in-blown leaves. But comfort was not forgotten. Some of them were for hot weather; they faced the north, were scarcely sunk, were little more than shady places. Some for the cold weather were deep hollows with southern exposure, and others for the wet were well roofed with herbage and faced the west. In one or other of these he spent the day, and at night he went forth to feed with his kind, sporting and romping on the moonlight nights like a lot of puppy Dogs, but careful to be gone by sunrise and safely tucked in a bed that was suited to the weather.

The safest ground for the Jacks was among the farms, where not only Osage hedges, but also the newly arrived barbed wire, made hurdles and hazards in the path of possible enemies. But the finest of the forage is nearer to the village among the truck farms—the finest of forage and the fiercest of dangers. Some of the dangers of the plains were lacking, but the greater perils of men, guns, Dogs, and impassable fences are much increased. Yet those who knew Warhorse best were not at all surprised to find that he had made a form in the middle of a market gardener's melon patch. A score of dangers beset him here, but there was also a score of unusual delights and a score of holes in the fence for times when he had to fly, with at least two score of expedients to help him afterward.

III

Newchusen was a typical Western town. Everywhere in it, were to be seen strenuous efforts at uglification, crowned with unmeasured success. The streets were straight level lanes without curves or beauty spots. The houses were cheap and mean structures of flimsy boards and tar paper, and not even honest in their ugliness, for each of them was pretending to be something better than itself. One had a false front to make it look like two stories, another was of imitation brick, a third pretended to be a marble temple.

But all agreed in being the ugliest things ever used as human dwellings, and in each could be read the owner's secret thought—to stand it for a year or so, then move out somewhere else. The only beauties of the place, and those unintentional, were the long lines of hand-planted shade trees, uglified as far as possible with whitewashed trunks and croppy heads, but still lovable, growing, living things.

The only building in town with a touch of picturesqueness was the grain elevator. It was not posing as a Greek temple or a Swiss chalet, but simply a strong, rough, honest grain elevator. At the end of each street was a vista of the prairie, with its farmhouses, windmill pumps, and long lines of Osage orange hedges. Here at least was something of interest—the gray green hedges, thick, sturdy, and high, were dotted with their golden mock oranges, useless fruit, but more welcome here than rain in a desert; for these balls were things of beauty, and swung on their long tough boughs they formed with the soft green leaves a color chord that pleased the weary eye.

Such a town is a place to get out of, as soon as possible, so thought the traveler who found himself laid over here for two days in late winter. He asked after the sights of the place; a white Muskrat stuffed in a case "down to the saloon"; old Baccy Bullin, who had been scalped by the Indians forty years ago; and a pipe once smoked by Kit Carson proved unattractive, so he turned toward the prairie still white with snow.

A mark among the numerous Dog tracks caught his eye; it was the track of a large Jackrabbit. He asked a passerby if there were any Rabbits in town.

"No, I reckon not. I never seen none," was the answer. A mill hand gave the same reply, but a small boy with a bundle of newspapers said, "You bet there is; there's lots of them out there on the prairie, and they come in town aplenty. Why, there's a big, big feller lives right round Si Kalb's melon patch—oh, an awful big feller, and just as black and as white as checkers!" and thus he sent the stranger eastward on his walk.

The big, big, "awful big" one was the Little Warhorse himself. He didn't live in Kalb's melon patch; he was there only at odd times. He was not there now; he was in his west-fronting form or bed, because a raw east wind was setting in. It was due east of Madison Avenue, and as the stranger plodded that way the Rabbit watched him. As long as the man kept the road the Jack was quiet, but the road turned shortly to the north, and the man by chance left it and came straight on. Then the Jack saw trouble ahead. The moment the man left the beaten track, he bounded from his form, and wheeling, he sailed across the prairie due east.

A Jackrabbit running from its enemy ordinarily covers eight or nine feet at a bound, and once in five or six bounds, it makes an observation hop, leaping not along, but high in the air, so as to get above all herbage and bushes and take in the situation. A silly young Jack will make an observation hop as often as one in four, and so waste a great deal of time. A clever Jack will make one hop in eight or nine, for observation. But Jack Warhorse as he sped, got all the information he needed, in one hop out of a dozen, while ten to fourteen feet were covered by each of his flying bounds. Yet another personal peculiarity showed in the trail he left. When a Cottontail or a Wood Hare runs, his tail is curled up tight on his back and does not touch the snow.

When a Jack runs, his tail hangs downward or backward, with the tip curved or straight, according to the individual; in some, it points straight down, and so, often leaves a little stroke behind the footmarks. The Warhorse's tail of shining black, was of unusual length, and at every bound, it left in the snow, a long stroke, so long that that alone was almost enough to tell which rabbit had made the track.

Now some Rabbits seeing only a man without any Dog would have felt little fear, but Warhorse, remembering some former stinging experiences with a far-killer, fled when the foe was seventy-five yards away, and skimming low, he ran southeast to a fence that ran easterly. Behind this he went like a low-flying Hawk, till a mile away he reached another of his beds; and here, after an observation taken as he stood on his heels, he settled again to rest.

But not for long. In twenty minutes his great megaphone ears, so close to the ground, caught a regular sound—*crunch, crunch, crunch*—the tramp of a human foot, and he started up to see the man with the shining stick in his hand, now drawing near.

Warhorse bounded out and away for the fence. Never once did he rise to a "spy hop" till the wire and rails were between him and his foe, an unnecessary precaution as it chanced, for the man was watching the trail and saw nothing of the Rabbit.

Jack skimmed along, keeping low and looking out for other enemies. He knew now that the man was on his track, and the old instinct born of ancestral trouble with Weasels was doubtless what prompted him to do the double trail. He ran in a long, straight course to a distant fence, followed its far side for fifty yards, then doubling back he retraced his trail and ran off in a new direction till he reached another of his dens or forms. He had been out all night and was very ready to rest, now that the sun was ablaze on the snow; but he had hardly got the place a little warmed when the *tramp, tramp, tramp* announced the enemy, and he hurried away.

After a half-mile run he stopped on a slight rise and marked the man still following, so he made a series of wonderful quirks in his trail, a succession of blind zigzags that would have puzzled most trailers; then running a hundred yards past a favorite form, he returned to it from the other side, and settled to rest, sure that now the enemy would be finally thrown off the scent.

It was slower than before, but still it came—*tramp, tramp, tramp.*

Jack awoke, but sat still. The man tramped by on the trail one hundred yards in front of him, and as he went on, Jack sprang out unseen, realizing that this was an unusual occasion needing a special effort. They had gone in a vast circle around the home range of the Warhorse and now were less than a mile from the farmhouse of the black Dog. There was that wonderful board fence with the happily planned hen hole. It was a place of good memory—here more than once he had won, here especially he had baffled the Greyhound.

These doubtless were the motive thoughts rather than any plan of playing one enemy against another, and Warhorse bounded openly across the snow to the fence of the big black Dog.

The hen hole was shut, and Warhorse, not a little puzzled, sneaked around to find another, without success, until, around the front, here was the gate wide open, and inside lying on some boards was the big Dog, fast asleep. The Hens were sitting hunched up in the warmest corner of the yard. The house Cat was gingerly picking her way from barn to kitchen as Warhorse halted in the gateway.

The black form of his pursuer was crawling down the far white prairie slope. Jack hopped quietly into the yard. A long-legged Rooster, that ought to have minded his own business, uttered a loud cackle as he saw the Rabbit hopping near. The Dog, lying in the sun, raised his head and stood up, and Jack's peril was dire. He squatted low and turned himself into a gray clod. He did it cleverly, but still might have been lost but for the Cat. Unwittingly, unwillingly, she saved him. The black Dog had taken three steps toward the Warhorse, though he did not know the Rabbit was there, and was now blocking the only way of escape from the yard, when the Cat came round the corner of the house, and leaping to a window ledge brought a flowerpot rolling down. By that single awkward act she disturbed the armed neutrality existing between herself and the Dog. She fled to the barn, and of course a flying foe is all that is needed to send a Dog on the warpath. They passed within thirty feet of the crouching Rabbit. As soon as they were well gone, Jack turned, and without even a "Thank you, Pussy," he fled to the open and away on the hard-beaten road.

The Cat had been rescued by the lady of the house; the Dog was once more sprawling on the boards when the man on Jack's trail arrived. He carried, not a gun, but a stout stick, sometimes called "dog medicine," and that was all that prevented the Dog attacking the enemy of his prey.

This seemed to be the end of the trail. The trick, whether planned or not, was a success, and the Rabbit got rid of his troublesome follower.

Next day the stranger made another search for the Jack and found, not himself, but his track. He knew it by its tail mark, its long leaps and few spy hops, but with it and running by it was the track of a smaller Rabbit. Here is where they met, here they chased each other in play, for no signs of battle were there to be seen; here they fed or sat together in the sun, there they ambled side by side, and here again they sported in the snow, always together. There was only one conclusion: this was the mating season. This was a pair of Jackrabbits—the Little Warhorse and his mate.

IV

[For a time the little Warhorse was a captive of men who raced him in competition with other rabbits—he outran, outfoxed, outmaneuvered them all. Eventually, a kind man who empathized with him secretly spirited him away and released him back in his old familiar rabbit country.]

For the moment the Little Warhorse gazed in doubt, then took three or four long leaps and a spy hop to get his bearings. Now spreading his national colors and his honor-marked ears, he bounded into his hard-won freedom, strong as ever, and melted into the night of his native plain.

He has been seen many times in Kaskado, and there have been many Rabbit drives in that region, but he seems to know some means of baffling them now, for, in all the thousands that have been trapped and corralled, they have never since seen the star-spangled ears of Little Jack Warhorse.

* * * * *

"Little Warhorse" by Ernest Thompson Seton, was included in Seton's Animal Heroes (New York: Charles Scribner's Sons, 1905). Ernest Thompson Seton (1860–1946) was born in South Shields, England. He moved to Canada in 1866 and later, to the United States. He is considered to be the founder of animal fiction writing as well as a prolific writer of nature stories. He was instrumental in founding the Boy Scouts of America and Woodcraft Indians. Wild Animals I Have Known and Animal Heroes are two of his bestsellers.

HERO IN FEATHERS

Ella A. Duncan

How little we know of the inner worlds of the rest of God's creation! We only know enough to marvel and wonder. With what wondrous qualities our Lord endowed even the lowliest of His creatures. Even a duck—Waddles.

* * * * *

When the doorbell rang that spring morning, two-year-old Susie found a small duck nestled in a basket on the front step. It was just a round, yellow ball of fluff with two black, shiny beads for eyes and a curious ebony bill that went poking about constantly into everything. It had always seemed extremely cruel to give children such small, helpless beings; too many such defenseless creatures are tortured to a slow death. Surely Susie would be no exception among children. John declared emphatically that the bit of down would be nothing but a nuisance; it was to be taken to the pet shop the next morning.

Then came the ordeal of separating one small, unreasoning being from another. From the moment she found him, all of Susie's other interests had been discarded for the tiny bit of quacking life. She was ecstatic when the duckling scrambled from his basket and waddled at her heels about the room. I tried to explain that he was just a baby duck and must go to his mother, but when I put him in a box on the back porch, Susie's howls from the front porch, and the duck's clatter, rent the air. We had to relent, but, of course, only temporarily.

Surprisingly, the little girl was gentle with the soft, fragile body of the duckling. As for him, from the very beginning there was no one else in the house but Susie. When she walked, he waddled at her heels; when she ran, he rolled over and over like an animated yellow tumbleweed, trying to keep up with her, and protesting such speed in high, hysterical quackings.

Susie spent hours, that first day, showing the birdlet her possessions. As the little girl displayed storybooks and blocks, the small duck nestled by her side, quacking contentedly. In her eagerness to make him understand, she bent her head to his level, chattering earnestly. In response, the yellow neck would stretch up and the beady eyes sparkle while the little duck talked in his own baby language. I have always thought that there is some canny or un-canny understanding between the young of the earth, something sadly im-possible between adult animals. Watching the little blond girl and the baby duck, I was sure that there was not only a sort of spiritual blending, but a definite mutual understanding of language. There was no doubt of it in the weeks and months that followed.

Within the first hour Susie named the duck. She chose "Waddles," truly an appropriate name for an embryo hero—but I anticipate.

It was raining the next morning, so it was easy to grant Waddles a day of reprieve. I think we knew then that he would never see the inside of a pet shop. Each morning after that we made feeble excuses for not sending him, until finally John exclaimed over his coffee, "Let's keep the little fellow. It would break Susie's heart to take him away now—besides, I sort of like him myself," he finished sheepishly.

At last Susie had a playmate—her first. There being no children her own age near us, she had been alone among adults all her short months on earth. There had been no name in Waddles' basket, so we never knew where he came from. I am sure, however, some friend much older and wiser than we must have brought him—someone who knew that everything on earth longs for something its own age, something with which to share like experiences and joys. To Susie and Waddles, everything on earth was still shiny new and wonderful beyond belief—things for exploring and exclaiming.

Together that summer in the high-fenced backyard, daughter and duck found a complete world of magic. To Ann, the maid, and to me, it was amazing how that funny little duck so quickly and completely took over what at times had been a real task for two adult human beings.

The two chased butterflies, built castles in the sandbox, played hide-and-seek among the shrubs and lawn furniture, or just sat in the sun and chattered about things beyond the ken of a grown-up world. There were hilarious games of their own invention, over which Susie went into spasms of laughter and Waddles quacked his glee in a voice that began to "change" as the summer wore on. His yellow down had given way to a thick coat of slate gray feathers, marked with black. Because we knew nothing of his ancestry, we had no way of knowing what his breed line might be. He grew to be larger than most ducks, however, and was a strong, handsome fellow as he waddled proudly about the yard, head and shoulders held high.

Waddles had been with us two years when Baby Carol came, and Susie was ready for nursery school. We brought the baby home from the hospital in her bassinet, and Ann went to call the two playmates from the backyard. They stood silently, side by side, for a few seconds, studying the new red-faced mite.

"Where are her teeth?" Susie wanted to know. But it was Waddles that surprised us most. Except for his various degrees of quacking, he had never made any other sound. Now he suddenly beat his great wings against his sides, let out a trumpeting honk, and sat down purposefully beside the bassinet. We did not know it then, but with that wild, foreign cry, Waddles was proclaiming to the world that he was at last an adult. On his shoulders had descended the grave responsibility of guard for a new, helpless being.

It was amusing, at first, to see the big duck there beside the bassinet, his neck held stiff and high, his keen black eyes darting in search of danger. Worn out from play with Susie, he had usually gone willingly to his box on the back porch. That night John had to pick him up and carry him—protesting and hissing—outside.

Early the next morning Waddles was at the back door, quacking urgently to be let in. After breakfast, to get rid of his infernal noise, I sent Susie out to play with him. Soon she was back. "He won't play with me anymore!" she wailed.

"It's the truth," said Ann. "He just ignored her." I was torn with sympathy for my eldest daughter in this first tragedy of life, and she was utterly bewildered by it. But before the week was over, a little boy and a little girl, near her age, moved into the neighborhood. Then came the glorious experience of nursery school—and Susie was no longer a baby.

As for Waddles, it finally seeped through his small duck brain that the only time his guarding act was necessary was when Baby Carol was put in the backyard for her sunbath. The rest of the day he waddled majestically about the yard, muttering philosophically to himself, or sat in the sun and brooded contentedly. The only time he resembled his former animated self was when the time for the sunbath drew near. He was always at the backdoor waiting. If Ann or I were late getting her out, he set up a demanding clatter. In a restrained frenzy of excitement, he would waddle beside the carriage until it was stopped. Then, always facing the house, he settled beneath it, every inch of his body at trained attention.

Once more, I was having reason to give thanks for Waddles as an aid to child rearing. It was impossible to teach Susie and her newfound friends to close the back gate as they should, but as long as Waddles was around neither man nor beast could come near his baby. The dogs and cats of the neighborhood soon learned to avoid that gate. Even the milkman asked if he might leave the milk at the front each morning, rather than battle the big duck.

It was Waddles himself I worried about at first. I was afraid he might get out and wander off, or be run over in the street. After the second venture up the driveway to the front of the house, however, he evidently decided that the outside world held little of interest for him. He returned to his big backyard and never again left it. It was his kingdom, and woe betide the trespasser!

It was that very vigilance, however, that nearly caused his banishment; I shudder yet to think how very near we came to disposing of him.

Because of an illness, Ann had to leave us, and a new girl was employed in her place. The first morning that she took the baby outside, Waddles flew at her in a veritable fury of beating wings, snapping beak, and clawing web feet. Before I could come to the rescue, he had ruined the girl's hose and left her legs bruised and bleeding. In shock and anger, she quit. Two others followed in quick succession. It was impossible for them to avoid the backyard entirely. It was even more impossible to convince Waddles that they were to become a part of the family. Up until then, he seemed to have had an uncanny instinct for doing as he should. We had never punished him, and I had no idea how to go about it now. The only solution seemed to be exile.

Then—miracle of miracles—Ann came back. All was peace in the backyard once again. I was not only thankful for that, and for her help, but a plague of rabies had broken out among the dogs of the town. Ann would guard the children as no strange girl could be expected to do, but we mothers lived in a nightmare of dread. We tried to cooperate in keeping the youngsters entertained, but it was difficult to restrain them.

One morning when there was no school, I had all the youngsters for a morning picnic. After the picnic Ann herded them into the house to get them ready for the moving pictures we were going to show. I took Baby Carol to the backyard for her belated nap. Making sure that the gate was closed and Waddles settled in his usual fighting stance beneath the carriage, I went back into the house. The phone rang. A friend down the street said, "I just saw a dog turn into your driveway, and if I know a mad dog, that one is."

Every time a stray dog had been seen in the neighborhood for weeks, everyone was sure it had rabies. Nevertheless, prickles of fright were breaking out along my spine. Then I thought, *The back gate—one of the children might have gone back for something.* On legs that threatened to buckle, I started for the yard. Before I was halfway through the house, for the second time in his life came that high, wild honk—and I *knew!*

Screaming for Ann, I burst through the back door upon a scene that will remain with me the rest of my days. Not three yards from the baby was a misshapen, shaggy dog with a swollen head, red, unfocused eyes, and dripping mouth. Flying to meet him was Waddles, wings

outspread and neck stretched forth, ebony beak snapping and cracking like a small, angry machine gun. I knew that Ann was close behind me with the broom; then I lost sight of everything, except the desire to gather my baby in my arms and race for safety.

Somehow I made it, with Ann and her broom as flanking support. She slammed the back door behind us and ran to call the police. Too weak and paralyzed with fear to move, I leaned against the closed door and listened to the uncanny battle outside. The blood-chilling growls and muttered barks of the mad dog told me that Waddles was doing his best, but I knew that his best was not going to be enough this time. I was too frightened to look, but from the sounds coming through the opened windows, the shaggy dog and the big duck were fighting all over the backyard. Their bodies bumped and threshed against the side of the house and porch; then, except for the slapping of Waddles' big wings, the snapping of his beak, and the duller sound of the dog's jaws, the fight would dim out. Waddles' first squawk of pain brought me to with the frenzied urge to do something.

"I can't just let him stay out there and fight alone when he doesn't have a chance!" I told Ann desperately.

"You certainly can't go out there and fight that mad dog bare-handed. Think of the children," she declared.

There was not a gun in the house, and the police could not possibly get there in time. I prayed that Waddles would somehow realize his danger and fly up on something out of reach before it was too late. But all the time I knew he would not. His stout little heart simply would not let him stop fighting until his enemy was driven from that yard. This time, however, his opponent lacked sense enough to flee, no matter what the punishment.

The pain-filled squawks and barks gradually lessened, as did the sound of the fight, until once again, all was quiet in the backyard. It was an ominous, deadly quiet, and through it Ann and I clung together until the police came.

There was a muffled shot in the back, then one of the officers came to the door. "I want you to see a sight you will never see again," he said.

The backyard was a shambles. Chairs had been upset. Flowers and shrubs were beaten down. Baby Carol's carriage had been overturned, and crisscrossing the sandbox, that had once held so much happiness for a small blond girl and a little duck, were dark red stains. In the open gateway, a wing tip touching the fence on either side, lay Waddles—his broken neck outstretched and ebony beak turned scarlet. Just beyond him, in the driveway, lay the body of the great yellow dog.

"I don't think the bullet was necessary," said the second officer, still absentmindedly holding his gun and looking with wonder at the mutilated head of the dog.

Somehow Waddles had managed to hold out until he drove his last enemy from the little plot of earth he held sacred and dear above all other. Some inborn instinct from his wild, dim past must have warned him that this mad invader meant death and destruction to everything he loved, and, like heroes the world over, he gave his life to preserve his little world and the happy way of life within it.

There were no medals or citations for Waddles—only a small grave in the corner of the yard he loved so well and the deep, undying devotion in the human hearts that knew him.

* * * * *

"Hero in Feathers," by Ella A. Duncan. Published November 1, 1949, in The Youth's Instructor. *Text printed by permission of Joe Wheeler (P.O. Box 1246, Conifer, CO 80433) and Review and Herald® Publishing Association, Hagerstown, MD 21740. If anyone has information regarding the author's next of kin, please send the information to Joe Wheeler. Ella A. Duncan wrote for popular and inspirational magazines around the middle of the twentieth century.*

THE GOOD LORD MADE THEM ALL
Series from compiler/editor Joe L. Wheeler

If you enjoyed reading
Spot, the Dog That Broke the Rules and Other Heroic Animal Stories
you'll want to read the other books in this superb series:

BOOK ONE: *Owney, the Post Office Dog*
and Other Great Dog Stories
Paperback, 160 pages. ISBN 13: 978-0-8163-2045-5
ISBN 10: 0-8163-2045-4

BOOK TWO: *Smoky, the Ugliest Cat in the World*
and Other Great Cat Stories
Paperback, 160 pages. ISBN 13: 978-0-8163-2121-6
ISBN 10: 0-8163-2121-3

BOOK THREE: *Wildfire, the Red Stallion*
and Other Great Horse Stories
Paperback, 160 pages. ISBN 13: 978-0-8163-2154-4
ISBN 10: 0-8163-2154-X

BOOK FOUR: *Dick, the Babysitting Bear*
and Other Great Wild Animal Stories
Paperback. 160 pages. ISBN 13: 978-0-8163-2221-3
ISBN 10: 0-8163-2221-X